DEATH ASKS THE QUESTION

Seemingly grand from the outside, the interior of Abner Hilton's house was a dilapidated, gloomy place — reflecting its morbid and desperately impoverished occupant. But Hilton's insane plan would lift him out of his poverty. He would murder his young niece, who was about to visit him; her dead father's will would ensure that her considerable wealth would pass to him. However, when his plan was put into operation, the young woman's horrifying death was to have terrifying repercussions . . .

JOHN RUSSELL FEARN

DEATH ASKS
THE QUESTION

Complete and Unabridged

LINFORD
Leicester

First published in Great Britain

First Linford Edition
published 2011

British Library CIP Data

Fearn, John Russell, *1908 – 1960.*
Death asks the question.- -
(Linford mystery library)
1. Nieces- -Death- -Fiction. 2 Murder- -
Fiction. 3. Horror tales.
4. Large type books.
I. Title II. Series
823.9′12–dc22

ISBN 978–1–44480–571–0

Published by
F. A. Thorpe (Publishing)
Anstey, Leicestershire

Set by Words & Graphics Ltd.
Anstey, Leicestershire
Printed and bound in Great Britain by
T. J. International Ltd., Padstow, Cornwall

This book is printed on acid-free paper

1

DEATH ASKS THE QUESTION

1

Fiend incarnate

The home of Abner Hilton was situated in a none-too populous region several miles from Philadelphia. It stood in solitary magnificence in its own grounds — a passably prosperous looking place, its nearest neighbours being a dozen similar homes at regular distances. To back and front there was nothing but wild, open country — the former looking over rugged moorland to a distant hill; the latter towards the smoky line on the horizon that denoted Philadelphia itself.

Within the dilapidated, depressing interior of the Hilton home, Abner Hilton sat scowling at his broken, dirty nails. The internal surroundings were as filthy as he was. Weak daylight filtering through the half-drawn Venetian blind glanced on faded, rotting wallpaper. It touched the spare furniture of the place, the most substantial article being an unusually long deal table provided with sloping wooden runnels on either side. In the room beyond, turned by the poor, half insane Hilton into a bedroom, the same drab daylight fell on muddy grey tangled sheets and dust caked floorboards. Gloom, depression — subhuman morbidity. All these things stalked the jetty shadows of the horrible place and filled both the rooms and Abner with a certain hellish meaning.

He was waiting — waiting for his young niece to visit him. He had not seen her since her childhood. She was worth a fortune in money and he wasn't worth a dime.

The thing to do then was to kill her, very skillfully, and throw the blame onto her fiancé Courtney Wayne, a young Philadelphian engineer. Once it was done he could have the money for himself under the will of his dead brother, the girl's father.

For months he had brooded over the idea in his rotting little retreat. She would come, surely. The outside of the house looked quite prepossessing. The neighborhood was fairly select and quiet. Finally he had written a letter. His one time culture had enabled him to write it very convincingly, expressing the urgent wish to see her and convey a confidential message that had been left in his keeping by her dead father.

Yes, it had been a very clever letter . . . And now he sat, a tattered, unshaven figure, eyes glowing with the unholy light of murder-lust — waiting, waiting. She would be here any time, now. For an instant his gaze shuttled to the battered alarm clock on the mantel; it was just three o'clock, the time appointed. That meant . . .

He jumped to his feet abruptly with a sharp and triumphant in-take of breath. There was a knock on the front door. The tap of a woman's hand, beyond doubt. Just the sort of tap Mary would give, he reflected. Dear, sweet child . . . He chuckled viciously to himself as he moved along the dusty hall, then flinging back the massive bolts he wrenched the door open.

5

His hungry little eyes flashed over a young woman modestly attired in a warm winter overcoat, golden hair peeping from beneath her hat. She was just as pretty as she'd been as a child, he decided. Not quite so luxurious in clothes as he had expected; there wasn't even a car visible in the drive. Evidently she had come by train to the local station . . . All these thoughts took perhaps two seconds as he surveyed her, then she started to speak — but he interrupted her with a raised, skinny hand, motioned inside the drab hall.

'Come in, my dear,' he invited gently, but to his irritation she drew away nervously.

'No — no, thank you. I only just wanted to know if — '

'Yes, yes, of course — I'm your Uncle Abner. Come along in.'

'But I — '

Hilton's lean jaws snapped together. There was no time for argument. Reaching forward suddenly he clutched the girl round the waist and flung his free hand over her mouth to stifle her cries of fright.

'You darned little fool!' he panted, dragging her within and slamming the door. 'Do you want the whole damned place to hear you? Why can't you do as your Uncle asks and — '

He stopped, momentarily surprised. The girl had fainted in his arms. For a moment he stood glaring down into her ashen face, then staggering beneath her weight he carried her into the living room and laid her on the long deal table.

Rubbing his skinny hands together he looked at her closely, puzzled for a while over the apparent cheapness of her clothing as he wrenched the overcoat from her unconscious form. For a girl worth a fortune she wasn't dressing half as well as he would have expected.

Still, that didn't matter — evidently the countryside was no place for finery. Besides, what did clothes matter anyhow? His main object was to be rid of her and put his predetermined plan into action.

Working with the swiftness of movements long rehearsed he tightly bound her wrists and ankles to the underside of the table legs. A piece of filthy rag thrust between her teeth and tied securely into position effectively gagged her. Another length of rope secured across her neck held her head tightly.

'A fortune, eh?' Hilton muttered, surveying her helplessly trussed form. 'We shall see, Mary, my dear . . . We shall see!'

Turning, he strode through the dimming daylight to the rickety sideboard and pulled a long carving knife and a saw from the left drawer. Gently he laid them down beside the girl, rubbed his palms softly together in ghoulish anticipation. Grunting impatiently he lighted an oil lamp and placed it on the hook over the table.

His actions were deliberate — the brutal, inhuman actions of a fiend.

First he sliced the knife down the girl's clothes, tore them away from her body then bedded them down in the empty fire grate. His cruel eyes rested for a while on her lissome nakedness under the dull lamp glow. Broken teeth glinted in a ghoulish smile as he found she had recovered consciousness and was trying desperately to raise her pinioned head.

'Oh, no, my dear,' he said gently, glaring into her terror stricken face. 'It is of little use trying to scream now — the gag will take care of that. It's my turn! Not a trace will remain by the time I'm finished with you. Mary Lillian Digby will vanish off the face of the earth!'

The girl struggled again, threshed and twisted as far as the ropes would permit, pulled her head upwards until the constriction of the cord set the veins bulging in her forehead. Then again she relaxed, dumb, staring blue eyes fixed on Hilton's grinning face. Suddenly he turned away and went into the adjoining kitchen, brought forth two large buckets and placed them at the ends of the table runnels.

Complacently he nodded, picked up the wickedly pointed knife — then drove it with all his strength between the girl's heaving breasts, gave it a left hand twist that struck clean through her heart.

There was a faint moan from behind the gag, then her struggles ceased. Blood began to well from the knife wound in her breast. Unmoved, Hilton smiled. With a steady hand he withdrew the blade and began to cut swiftly, hacked and carved until at last he had removed the heart itself. Eyes bright with madness he laid the bluish organ gently to one side, sucked breath over his broken teeth in sadistic glee.

Again he returned to the mangled thing that had been a young woman. He worked ceaselessly until perspiration drenched him from head to foot, worked to the sound of blood dripping from the runnels into the buckets. Time and time again he traveled with them into the filthy kitchen and emptied them into a tub.

So, little by little, he dismembered the body, cut away the legs, arms and head, left only a bleeding torso with a gaping ragged hole where the heart had been torn out. Panting hard from his exertions he stared at the dismembered organ.

'At least you can never beat again!' he muttered. 'Not even in a dead body! It is safer with the heart removed — detached . . . '

He brooded over that, then suddenly looked up with a start as there came a heavy pounding on the front door. For an instant he hesitated, staring at the pulped mess on the table. Then quickly wiping his hands on a filthy rag he sped through the crawling shadows of the hall and opened the door gently. The dying light fell on a young, well-dressed man with a clean-shaven face and determined blue eyes.

'Well, what do you want?' Hilton demanded irritably.

'You Abner Hilton, sir?'

'Certainly I am. What of it?'

'I believe Mary came along to see you this afternoon? I saw her come in as a matter of fact, a little while ago. I thought I might as well join her. I'm Courtney Wayne, her fiancé.'

'Oh, I see!' Hilton's face lighted with sudden understanding. In the gloom the young man failed to notice the subtle craftiness that crept into it. 'Pray come in, young man — I've rather been expecting you. You must excuse the dim light but unhappily the current is off — a fuse, you know. I'm an old man and don't know much about these things.'

'Maybe I can fix it for you, sir,' Wayne

remarked, and stepped into the shadows.

The instant he did so fear crawled through him. The damp, odorous air was heavy with the reek of human blood; the whole place stank like an offal dump. Abner Hilton felt his powerful young hand close on his arm.

'Where is Mary, sir?' his voice demanded from the dark.

'Right ahead,' the old man chuckled. 'We were talking in the lamplight, owing to the fuse. Go on — right ahead down the passage to that door there. You can see the light.'

Wayne hesitated for a moment, then obeyed. In a few moments he gained the open doorway and started into the dreary surroundings. Instantly his eyes alighted on that ghastly horror on the table. The room was like a charnel house; the glow of the softly swinging oil lamp in the hall draft cast its dimness on things that sent his appalled mind tumbling madly in the depths of hell.

'Mary!' he screamed insanely. 'Oh, God! I'm mad! That can't be my Mary there — '

'That *is* Mary,' Hilton informed him, closing the door softly and moving towards the fireplace. 'Mary — or what remains of her! You didn't expect it, did you? Thanks for coming like this — it's saved me the trouble of sending for you.'

Wayne's voice cracked in hysterical horror and fury over the words ripped from his lips.

'You fiend! You filthy, murdering devil! You've killed her — even dismembered her body — mutilated her face! Oh, God, why didn't I get here sooner — '

'That is Mary, but *you* killed her!' Hilton said tonelessly. 'I will arrange that later — '

He broke off as Wayne made a sudden violent leap towards him. It was the very action he had been expecting. Instantly his hand came up from behind his back and was revealed as clutching the heavy iron poker from the grate.

Wayne never realized clearly what happened, as he pitched senseless to the filthy, blood spattered floorboards . . .

2

Heartbeats of the Slain

Wayne returned to his senses with the realization that he was firmly bound to the heavy old-fashioned fire grate. His eyes, blurred with the pain from his damaged head, stared drunkenly at the dancing, leering face of Abner Hilton in the lamp glow.

With a low snarling laugh the old man came forward, shook his skinny fist malevolently.

'I waited until you recovered, young man,' he said throatily. 'I wanted you to see everything right through to the end! You might as well — the police will want to accuse you.' He went closer, hot foetid breath blowing in Wayne's face.

'Do you realize what I'm going to do to you, Courtney? I intend to break your will — turn you by slow degrees into an imbecile! By torture — by mental anguish, by whatever means I can and as soon as I can! Clever, isn't it? And well worth it!

'You see, with you and Mary both out of the way — you as her murderer, in a fit of insanity, it leaves only me to collect. So good of you to follow Mary here. Now watch!'

Wayne didn't answer. He felt already that his mind was on the verge of cracking under the physical pain and the added horror of gazing. Yet gaze he did, with fascinated nausea, as the inhuman Hilton continued his work.

The knife carved flabbily into the unresisting flesh of the thing that had been a woman; the saw grated viciously over bone. Every sound of it went through Wayne's body and brain as though he were the victim.

By slow degrees through what seemed endless hours he saw the corpse carefully cut up into pieces and thrust into a heavy sack. Then Hilton became fiercely active. Lifting the buckets of blood he vanished into the kitchen and there came the sound of running tap water. When he returned he was rubbing his hands complacently.

'So easy to dilute the blood to the consistency of weak dye and pour it down the sink,' he breathed venomously. 'That is what the police will find you did! I will tell them that. You cut the body into sections and made it unrecognizable, hoping for the perfect crime. The remains will be buried in the garden. Remember that!'

So saying he seized the sack and pulled it along the floorboards to the back door, leaving behind him a smear of blood that deeply stained the boards. Wayne watched glassily, stunned with horror. He would not, could not believe that he was seeing all that remained of Mary being carried away in that sack.

He screamed at the thought — raved and cursed with impotent, helpless fury, wrenched and tore at his ropes with the ferocity of a madman but all to no purpose.

Thirty minutes later Hilton returned, the sweat of exertion dewing his lean, brutal face.

'Hard work, digging,' he said ominously. 'She's well bedded down — a good four feet. And when she went down my chances of inheritance went up. Understand? Say something, you idiot — say something!' He struck him savagely in the face with the flat of his hand, but Wayne remained silent. His mind was utterly numbed.

In a daze he watched the old man complete the details — watched him clean the table and floorboards with caustic, swab out the pails, and then set fire to the clothes in the grate. Turning at last from the glowing ashes he indicated the bloodstained knife and saw laid carefully on one side.

'Evidence! He breathed maliciously. 'Evidence when the Police come — evidence that you did it! You killed Mary Lillian Digby!'

Wayne remained mute; his head drooped between his shoulders with the heaviness of unconsciousness. Hilton went forward and examined him closely, convinced himself it was not a trick. Only then did he loosen the ropes, seize the young man by the shoulders and drag him into the filthy, dark apartment that had once been a second drawing room.

Working swiftly he rebound his ankles and wrists — spread-eagled him on the barren floor. Skipping back into the kitchen he brought hammer and massive curved staples, fastened the ropes around them then drove them deep into the boards.

'Guess that'll hold you,' he muttered, reflecting — then again he went to the kitchen and presently returned with a large can of water, slightly punctured in the base to permit of the water dripping through drop by drop.

With fiendish ingenuity he fastened it to the old electric light fixture above, carefully arranged it so that the drops fell steadily on the forehead of the pinioned, unconscious man.

Torture — absolute and vicious — torture calculated to break a man's mind, not from pain but from the agonizing anticipation of each icy drop through endless hours.

The intense gratification at the thing he

had done did not abate in Abner Hilton the next day. After a few hours of sleep — remarkably peaceful considering the inhuman brutality of his crime — he entered the second drawing room to survey his prisoner, dimly visible in the light drifting through the chinks in the drawn Venetian blind.

He found Wayne conscious again, still tightly bound on the floor, face drawn into tight, weary lines of suffering, water dripping down it from the almost empty can over his head.

'You — you inhuman fiend!' He muttered the words thickly. 'You devil! Do you think you can get away with this?'

'I know I can,' Hilton replied affably, rubbing his hands. 'I'm sorry I can't make the room warmer — unfortunately there is no fireplace in here. Nor can I offer to release you.'

Wayne glared at him dully. His body was already numbed and stiff from his immovable position and the icy draft blowing under the door. Only his head seemed to have feeling, felt near the bursting point with the leaden dropping of the icy cold water, more searing than molten metal. His jagged nerves were keyed into intense agony of expectancy for every drop.

'Sorry, too, that I can't offer you anything to eat just yet,' Hilton went on sardonically. 'I have little to spare, but I'll see you get enough to keep you alive until the police come. Water, though, you can have in plenty,' he added grimly. With that he went out and refilled the can, put it back in place, and left the tortured man to himself again.

So, throughout the day, Wayne suffered exquisite tortures, he felt his mind slipping little by little under the terrible strain. Abner Hilton waited in fiendish expectancy for something to happen — but nothing did.

He had expected inquiries for both Wayne and Mary, but neither came. Instead a host of invisible presences seemed to watch him silently in dire and horrible reproach for the sin on his soul. Most of the fears he dismissed with a sneering grin on his feral lips.

Once he glanced through the rear

kitchen window towards the spot where he had buried Mary's remains, and beheld it untouched. Then he returned to commune with himself in the shadows.

Late in the afternoon he moved into the second drawing room, cut Wayne's limbs free from the staples but nonetheless kept him securely bound.

'I'm going to be merciful to you,' he said thickly, delivering a kick in his aching ribs. 'I'm giving you a respite; tomorrow I'll resume the treatment. In the end I'll break you!

'When the police come I'll say it was you who attacked both Mary and me. Understand!' His bitter little eyes glared in the flickering light of the lamp in his gnarled hand, hurled mental suggestions into the torture-weary mind of the man sprawling on the floor . . . All ideas of escape were stillborn in Wayne's brain. He could hardly even think, so overcome was he by exhaustion.

Hilton left him at last and so, for two more days, the ghastly business went on. Wayne was alternately tortured and released, given only enough meagre food and water to keep him alive in order that he would be able to speak when the law finally caught up.

And, just as Hilton had hoped, he was hardly master of his own will any longer — almost did believe by the endless hours of implacable hypnotism the old man indulged in that he *had* killed Mary. The horror of her death and the continued torture had become a crushing obsession slowly warping his mind.

Only at times was he aware of himself, realizing with leaden helplessness that nobody would be concerned about his disappearance. He had been on a vacation from his normal work in any case and only Mary knew. Mary! Merciful God!

It was on these occasions of self-assertion however that he tried with pained weariness to work free of the ropes holding his wrists. The staples holding them were fairly rough; in time he might break through his bonds. But it would take days.

On the third night, puzzled by the continued absence of action, Hilton went to bed early, lay awake gazing at the darkened, chilly room. Then at last he turned on his side amidst the dirty sheets and closed his eyes.

The silence was still disturbing him — even Wayne in the adjoining room was curiously quiet, working silently and laboriously in the dark on the ropes that held him, flaying away the tough thickness little by little with muscles that were cracked and aching.

Then, as he lay silent. Hilton heard something. There crept into his senses a dull, ticking sound, heavy with apparent distance.

Tick — tick — tick.

With the measured beat of a metronome, gradually becoming louder. Very slowly creeping up by imperceptible degrees, until at last the faded walls of the entire room groaned with the pulsating mystery.

Thud — thud. Thud — thud. Rhythmic, insistent, inhuman.

At last Hilton sat bolt upright in the bed. One skinny hand clutched the dirty tattered shirt that served as night attire. Staring wildly into the gloom he listened with twitching face muscles to the still resolute beating, for all the world like a gigantic human heart.

Heart? That thought knifed into his rotten brain. Instantly his memory was transferred to the heart he had cut out of the girl. He had cut it out to be sure life could never return, and now —

Clammy sweat drenched him as he listened. His breath rasped over his stumpy teeth. There was no way of telling exactly where that awful sound was coming from. It might be to one side, above or below — he could not determine. It seemed to fill all space.

Throb, throb, throb . . .

'No!' he shouted hoarsely, leaping out of the bed. 'No! *Stop!*'

And instantly the sound ceased!

The whole house seemed to become mute, horribly silent after the torturing rhythm of the beating.

With dragging footsteps and sweat-drenched face Hilton moved to the adjoining room and twisted the door key with trembling fingers. All was quiet within. Wayne lay like a log in the dim gloom, stirred only slightly as a match flared in Hilton's quaking hand. The old man's hoarse voice came to him.

'Courtney, you heard it?' he demanded thickly. 'You heard that beating?'

'I heard nothing,' Wayne muttered dully, and relaxed again.

For a moment the old man stood gazing at him, then he went out. Wayne lay silent for a while after he had gone, wondering what he had been talking about. He certainly had heard nothing. Then once more he set to work on the laborious task of fraying through his ropes.

In the meantime Hilton returned to his room and waited a long time in the shadowed gloom, but the mysterious sound was not repeated. At last recovering some of his courage he climbed into bed, nerves tensed for a recurrence of the sound.

Presently he heard it, very soft and low, that measured beat sweeping up from nowhere.

Louder and louder became the ticking, mad, nerve-racking tempo. Hilton shot out of bed once more, again screamed for it to stop — and as before it obeyed. Weakly he staggered to the front hall door and opened it, stared out toward the dimness of the drive.

Slowly he crept outside and looked about him, down past the many rear outhouses with their sloping roofs. There was nothing unusual visible — only a quiet, dark immensity.

He knew not how long he stood shivering in the night breeze. His next clear remembrance was of being back in his bedroom. He crawled back onto the bed at last and lay in frigid horror for the return of the beating — but the night passed quietly and he awoke again to the gray glimmerings of an ashy dawn.

3

Why Did You Kill Me?

Shaken by the experience of the night Abner Hilton felt like a trapped animal. Though he did not believe in the supernatural, though he inwardly boasted that he had no conscience, he could not altogether rid himself of the remembrance of his crime. Time and time again the vision of the slain girl rose up before him.

In his mind he could again hear the sloughing of the knife as it carved her flesh, the grate of the saw against her bones.

He scraped together a scanty meal and then went in to his prisoner with a few crusts and some water. Wayne looked at him dully, but behind his back his hands were slowly pulling away the remainders of his frayed rope. A night of rubbing on the floor staple nearest to him had cut

27

them through. They gave way just as Hilton was bending towards him.

Instantly his fingers closed round the old man's skinny throat, sent the meagre meal hurtling through the air. Hilton was pulled down to the floor with Wayne's fingers crushing hard into his leathery neck.

Wayne wished desperately he could get to his feet, but his bound ankles prevented it. His only hope lay in strangling the old man where he was — but in that he was doomed to failure. With a sudden vicious twist Hilton wriggled sideways, brought round his foot with all his strength and kicked Wayne violently in the ribs.

He gasped with the sudden pain, desisted in his effort to get to his feet — and in that moment Hilton acted. He had the advantage in every way. Wayne was bound and weak from his ordeal; Hilton was free and furiously energetic.

'So you thought you'd escape, eh?' he breathed venomously. 'You thought you'd fool me, huh? Well you won't!'

With that he dived away and snatched

up the heavy, dirty plate on which he had brought the food. Even as Wayne tried to get up the plate came down on his head with stunning force, edgewise. He sank down mutely, blood streaming from a scalp cut.

'It was you who plotted that heart beating stunt!' Hilton screamed. 'You! I don't know how, but you did it! You'll not do it again, Courtney. Damn you, no! I'll kill you first!'

Savagely he rebound his victim's ropes, spread-eagled him back in his old position. Then he refilled the can and stood looking at the unconscious figure in vicious glee.

'You can stay that way until I want you! Without food and without water — at least to drink! No more leniency — no more leniency!'

And with that he stamped fiercely from the room, slammed and locked the door.

Only once did he return, and that was towards evening. Wayne was half-conscious, muttering supplications for release. The old man's feral lips twisted in an unholy smile; his only response was to make sure the water can was refilled then he went into his bedroom to pass the night.

But the instant he entered the gloomy shoddiness — for the oil in his lamp was exhausted — he felt a strange fear clawing at his heart. The memory of the night before returned to him. He sat on the bed edge, listening with one ear half cocked for some sound of the heart, but instead there came something else, something that sent the blood crawling in streams of ice through his withered body.

'Abner Hilton, why did you kill me?'

The merest whisper, an ice-cold question that seemed to creep from the Unknown. It started Hilton's heart racing madly, set crawling fingers of ghastly fear clutching at his vitals.

'*Abner Hilton, why did you kill me?*'

It was stronger this time — a woman's voice calling softly, from an incredible distance. As in the beating of that enigmatic heart it was impossible to guess the exact source of the sound.

'Why did you kill me?' Words dreary with anguished reproach.

He leaped savagely to his feet and

stared madly round him in the dimness. Viciously he struck a match, but the flickering light revealed no change. It went out and scorched his fingers.

'Imagination!' he panted hoarsely. 'Imagination — or nerves!'

'No, Abner Hilton — neither imagination or nerves, but the voice of the woman you killed,' the voice answered sombrely.

'You slew me, carved my body into pieces and buried the remains! You tore out the heart — but in the heart there is not life — only in the mind. The mind lives on. In the end I will destroy you, as you destroyed me!'

With a pallid face he listened to the words, heart racing agonizedly against his skinny ribs. *Her* voice — the voice of Mary Lillian Digby — speaking from hell knew where!

Suddenly he found relief in action. As before he made straight for the second drawing room and stared in palsied fear at the bound figure of Wayne. He certainly was not responsible.

Mad with fright he left him and

blundered outside into the half clouded moonlight, glared about the sodden grounds of his home with the eyes of a maniac. Just as on the previous night there was nothing to disturb the aching quiet.

Breathless, shaking with fear, he returned inside at last, bolted the heavy front door with fingers that were oddly brittle. Cold seeping waves of superstitious fear were clawing at his evil heart.

As he tottered uncertainly down the hall, striking match after match to allay the crushing dark, he tried to convince himself that it was all imagination. That he hadn't heard anything. It was some trick of Courtney Wayne's; it *had* to be!

He twisted round and fumbled along to the second drawing room again, passed inside and examined the spread-eagled man closely, was forced to admit as before that he was *not* responsible. He was a silent, stupefied man, water trickling down his ashen face from the slowly dripping can.

Very quietly Hilton withdrew again into the abysmal dark of the hall, nearly wept with rage and fear as he found his matches were exhausted. Weakly, knees like jelly, he clawed his way back into the main living room and stood for a while in the jetty gloom, eyes staring at the hazy gray oblong where the window lay.

Turning he searched for the rickety chair and dropped his leaden limbs into it. Spittle was drooling unheeded from his quivering lips; sweat drenched his skinny body. The complete ghastly fear of a supernatural unknown had him in its grip.

For nearly an hour he sat there and heard nothing. A blank nothing that hemmed him in like a living, avenging presence. The only sound he once detected was a long drawn out groan, which he knew came from Courtney Wayne as he returned to consciousness.

A third look at the bound man convinced him; he was still there in the very dim moonlight filtering through the blind. In some odd way he was glad of the man's presence; it did something to alleviate the terrible fear numbing his being.

An hour later quivering, brain-numbing reaction set in. With heavy feet he scraped along to his bed and lay face down upon it, trying to muffle his ears to the dreaded sound he was afraid to hear. Softly, gently, came the resumed beating of that heart — and above it the awful, sepulchral voice.

'Abner Hilton, it is dark and cold in the grave you dug for me! I cannot rest. I am returning to life, to the land of mortals, to ask you face to face why you killed me! I am not dead, Abner Hilton. *I am alive!* Listen to the beat of the heart you cut away! Listen to it, gathering power!'

Shaking like an aspen Hilton listened — could not help himself. The voice ceased and the subdued rhythm of the heart became swifter, louder.

Pat, pat, pat, pat . . .

'You hear, Abner Hilton?' the voice breathed. 'I live! I have come back from the grave to ask why you killed me! Look in my grave! Dig down deep and you will find I have gone! Dig! *Dig!*'

4

The Remains Walk!

Hilton could stand it no longer. With a desperate scream he leaped out of the bed, blundered through the dark to the kitchen, felt round frantically until he encountered the handle of his shovel. Panting hard he wrenched back the outer door and charged madly into the garden outside, plowing heavily through rank soaking weeds and grass to the clear soil space where he had put, Mary's butchered remains.

With savage desperate movements born of ghastly fear he drove the blade into the earth, shovelled the soil to one side. He worked with mechanical frenzy until the blood pounded insanely through his veins and drove his heart to erratic spurts of beating.

On and on he shoveled, flinging the loose earth away with the ease of a maniac, until at last his spade ploughed through the sack in which he had placed the remains. Shaking with fright and exertion he pulled it free, gazed with stupid eyes as it moved drearily in the night breeze.

It was indeed empty! The remains had gone!

'No!' he muttered desperately. 'No — no, it can't be! I'm going mad! I know I'm going mad! You couldn't rise from the grave! You were utterly destroyed — dismembered! You — '

He stopped, the sack falling from his nerveless fingers. The moon, which had been shining diffusedly through ragged clouds suddenly emerged from their midst with a pale and leprous glow, cast its pale silver over the unkempt grounds and the hole of the grave.

But it was to none of these things that Hilton's mind was directed — his fixed, incredulous eyes were chained to a figure walking slowly towards him along the uneven ground.

It appeared to be the naked figure of a woman, arms extended towards him! And as she came nearer he could behold quite clearly against the whiteness of her skin the black marks at the joints of her legs and arms where he had cut them from the body! One other, round the base of the neck, held him mute.

Making hardly any sound she quietly advanced, coming nearer and nearer, and still he stood paralyzed with numbing shock.

'Abner Hilton, you killed me!' she said at last, in the same dreary grave-ridden voice he had heard in the house. 'I have come back — to ask you why you did it!'

Within six feet of him she stopped, a lovely but forlorn figure, hair moving slightly in the mild wet wind. Clearly he could distinguish the graceful curves of her body, the rounded formations of her breasts — but upon one of them was a dark patch — a hole where he had torn out the heart to make sure she would never come back.

Never come back! That realization burst in his diseased mind like a bolt of living fire. He found action at last in a desperate, piercing scream, turned swiftly and went blundering and gasping over the uneven ground — anything to escape the woman who had risen to question her fate.

Even as he flew over the ground, driven by insane terror, he could hear feet racing after him — not the sound of woman's feet but the heavy clomping of a nightmare creature.

Thud, thud, thud, like the beating heart he had heard.

He threw himself screaming through the front doorway, into the hall. His fingers twisted the key of the second drawing room door and he went flying inwards to hurl himself beside the silent figure of Wayne.

'Courtney, in God's name save me!' he screamed frantically. 'Save me! She's come back! Mary's come back from the grave!' His trembling fingers wrenched a penknife from his pocket, slashed through the ropes holding the tortured man. 'Save me, Courtney! Say you will! It's Mary!'

That jerked something of consciousness into Wayne's leaden brain. He stared into the dark, down, at the dim, pawing, gulping figure on the floor beside him. Stiffly he tried to move to his feet — then his eyes jerked round at the sound of feet in the hall. A light was bobbing along it.

Cold terror surged through him too as in the doorway he beheld the same naked woman's figure that Hilton had seen — a woman who stared tensely, wounds on her rejoined limbs clearly visible. Almost at the same moment the owner of the storm lantern became visible, pushed the woman to one side and charged forward, clutched the screaming Hilton round the neck.

In the light of the storm lantern on the floor Wayne dazedly watched what took place, saw a powerful shouldered man with a face of frozen hate clutch Hilton's skinny throat in sinewy fingers, crush into it with all the strength at his command.

'Kill my daughter, eh?' His bitter voice knifed in the quiet. 'Cut her up, would you? My Annie! By God, you filthy butcher, this is where you go to the hell you deserve!'

Hilton tried to speak but the compressing fingers would not let him. His miserable body threshed madly on the floor. Slowly but surely his struggles became weaker and at last ceased altogether.

Only then did the man rise up and kick the corpse violently with his heavy shod foot, turned, then stared at Wayne in amazement.

'You're alive!' he shouted hoarsely — and with his words the girl in the doorway seemed to arise from her horrific trance and advanced at a run.

Wayne felt convinced in that moment that he was going insane at last — for the girl *was* Mary! There could be no mistaking her face. Mary, yes — naked, with scars of her hideous death still upon her. Mary!

His lips moved to utter her name then even as her white arms reached towards him he relapsed into darkness and brief rest.

Wayne realized as he came back to consciousness that he could only have been senseless a few minutes. He was lying on his back, all his ropes removed, the face of Mary and her rugged-faced companion bending over him. The only change was that she was now wrapped in an overcoat.

'Courtney, dear — Courtney!' she breathed, gathering him into her arms. 'Thank God you're alive! I thought you were dead — that was why I helped Craven here.'

Dazedly, weakly, Wayne raised himself on one elbow and stared toward the light of the lantern.

'What — what's it all about?' he asked helplessly. 'I saw you cut in pieces by that fiend, Mary — I saw it! A moment ago you were naked; I saw the marks.'

The girl smiled faintly. 'Only tights, Courtney, marked on the joints with black paint. Cold, yes — but the only way to drag this fiendish uncle of mine into the open.'

'Come to think of it, I didn't see your face when — when Hilton butchered you,' Wayne shuddered. 'It was utterly unrecognizable, and . . . '

'It isn't really so complicated as it seems, sir,' the man muttered. 'This filthy devil intended to kill Miss Digby here, but instead he killed my girl Annie. She was canvassing this district for radio set orders. We had got a little business together and were doing quite well.'

'Actually, Courtney,' Mary intervened; 'although I said in my letter to you that I was coming to see Uncle, I changed my mind at the last moment. It seems that Mr. Craven's daughter arrived at almost the time for my appointment. Evidently Uncle didn't give her the chance to speak, and not having seen me for years he mistook poor Annie for me, both of us being fair and young.'

'That must have been it,' Wayne nodded drearily. 'As for myself I was afraid for you and came to see if I could help you when you visited your uncle. There wasn't time to come to your home first, so I came straight here. I saw somebody like you enter the house whilst I was still a distance away; after that I came in and saw ... ' He stopped, brokenly.

Mary slowly nodded 'I got worried when I couldn't get any news of you. All I could find out was that you'd started on a holiday. Closer inquiry, though, revealed that you'd followed me here.

'I decided to come here after all and it was evening when I arrived; that was the evening after I should have come, of course. The first person I ran into was Mr. Craven in the grounds. He had just dug up some remains out of a sack — '

'I'd found that Annie had last been seen at this place,' Craven muttered bitterly. 'I found bloodstains on the grass and traced them to that newly dug hole. I identified the remains as those of Annie — there were certain birthmarks on her body that only I knew about. It was she all right.

'Well, I couldn't see any real motive for the brutality until Miss Digby happened upon me; then I began to see what had happened — how my poor girl had got what was intended for somebody else. It seemed pretty evident that you had probably gone the same way since you had disappeared.

'Both of us wanted vengeance on the old fiend and were prepared to go to any lengths to exact it.'

'And yet you didn't go to the police?' Wayne asked wonderingly.

'Police!' derided Craven contemptuously. 'What could they do? Just give this devil here the hot seat for murder. That wasn't enough for me — I wanted to torture him as he had tortured my poor girl — I wanted to drive him mad with my own efforts. Miss Digby felt pretty much the same way about your disappearance. Of course, we had no guarantee that you really were dead, but we suspected it as the only explanation. The best way to find out was to get Hilton out of the house and look for ourselves — and that demanded something pretty ingenious. We managed it, between us.'

He paused and smiled reminiscently. 'Being a radio engineer came in handy,' he went on grimly. 'I got a microphone and small loudspeaker and lowered them by wire half way down the main chimney breast.

'I knew that in common with all houses of this old type the main fireplace flues would end in one chimney, so the sound would travel to all rooms possessing a fireplace. It was fairly certain Hilton would occupy such a room. It was easy to get to the roof by the outhouses, without much noise either.

'Once that was done Miss Digby and I went to our apparatus, just beyond the range of the back grounds. The microphone in the chimney picked up every sound that Hilton made; with headphones we could visualize his movements. Every time he went to bed the mattress springs squeaked. As to the voice of the woman it was Miss Digby herself speaking into our own microphone, which of course emanated from the loudspeaker in the chimney. The heart effect was simply a ticking alarm clock, made louder or quieter by a volume control on the microphone.'

Wayne nodded slowly. 'I begin to see now why Hilton was so frantic. For myself I heard nothing; this room has no fireplace. Besides, I was unconscious most of the time.'

'When he shouted for the beats to stop we naturally obeyed the order, hearing him distinctly,' Craven breathed. 'That got him! He really thought the devil was after him. Just the same we didn't tempt him out the first night; he needed time to think and work himself up into a real frenzy of fright.

'We did that tonight, of course. Miss Digby joined me again after sundown, complete with an outfit that looked like my girl risen from the grave. The rest you know. Of course it was I who took away my poor Annie's remains.'

'And you?' Wayne asked slowly. 'You've murdered Hilton. That is against the law, fiend or not.'

Craven shrugged his heavy shoulders and looked down at the corpse.

'I'm going to give myself up and trust to the mercy of the law. With your evidence too and my dead girl's remains where is the jury which would convict?'

'We'll back you to the end,' Wayne said quietly, getting to his feet with difficulty.

The girl's arm went round him supportively as she helped him from the drab house. As they passed into the cool night air they looked away to the east.

Ragged dawn was already creeping over the misty, saturated countryside. Somewhere amidst it perhaps, abandoned and alone, was the fiendish soul of Abner Hilton . . .

2

FOOLPROOF

Judge Rufus Langton sat alone in the library of his small hunting lodge at Railsby Bend. The heavy law book in his hands, the soft cone of light from the desk-lamp, the dark walnut of the shadowed room, were things apart from the raging fury of the winter storm outside.

Only rarely did he glance up. The book was good reading. But he had to keep his eye on the clock. His son and daughter-in-law were due any time, roads permitting

The whining of the wind, the slashing cut of the rain down the long window panes, effectually muffled from him the slight sound of the nearest window catch being lifted with a knife blade. He only became aware of his seclusion being disturbed when the black velvet curtains suddenly billowed inwards and a blast of icy wind surged into the warmth of the room.

Instantly he was on his feet, bewildered, his first thought being that the gale had snapped the window catch. He soon saw how wrong he was as he beheld a figure standing in the opening, a figure in dripping mackintosh and sodden felt hat. An automatic was gripped tightly in his hand.

'Make no moves, Judge Langton! Sit down!'

Langton's legal brain registered the situation instantly. He tightened his lips, dropped into a chair with hands upraised. The intruder reached rearwards, shut the window, then came forward slowly. He stopped when the desk-light glinted somberly on the gun.

'You don't know me, do you? His voice was low-pitched, merciless.

Judge Langton shook his iron-grey head. He was trying to place the lean, rigidly set face, the resolute jaw, the darkly smoldering eyes, the whipcord body.

'No, I don't know you.' he muttered, his voice calm. 'And I wish you'd come in by the door instead of upsetting me like this. You can put that gun away, too. I am alone, and quite unarmed.'

'You think I don't know that?' his visitor asked laconically. 'I have kept a tally on your movements for months, Langton — and now you are going to get what's owing to you. Understand?'

Langton's powerful face set into grim lines. He peered again into the shadows.

'Who the devil are you, anyway?'

The man sat down in the chair opposite and held his gun steady on the desk edge. 'My name's Joseph Gell,' he replied slowly. 'Does that stir anything in your memory?'

'Gell? Gell?' Langton frowned reflectively, slanted his eyes to the desk drawer containing his own revolver, then shook his head. 'I guess it doesn't. I don't seem to — Wait a minute!' he broke off. 'Gell! Somebody of that name was condemned to death a couple of years ago. Peter Rayburn Gell. Convicted of murder in the first degree.'

The visitor nodded slowly, and raindrops spattered on the blotter from his sodden hat.

'Right!' he acknowledged grimly. 'Your memory isn't so bad, at that. Peter Gell was my son. He took the rap because the high-ups responsible for the mess wouldn't come into the open. They left him holding the bag — and you condemned him. Remember?'

'He was convicted of murder,' Langton retorted. 'Foul murder, Gell. He killed a woman and a man in cold blood. He openly admitted it; and he got the full penalty.'

'He died,' Gell said slowly, 'because he followed orders and wouldn't squeal, a fact which you and that damned jury didn't — or else wouldn't — take into account.

You guys on the side of justice, so called, have a law that says 'a life for a life.' You might as well know that we fellers on the other side have a law that works out the same way — only sometimes we're a bit longer enforcing it! I say you killed my boy just as if you'd murdered him. You knew the real culprits, but you wouldn't stir yourself to bring them into court.'

Langton smiled frozenly. 'Whatever they did, whoever they were, your son had to answer for his individual crimes! He confessed to murder, and was executed . . . You're not the first one, by any means, who has tried to get at me for the sentences I've given out — '

'Shut up!' Gell ordered. 'You're doing the listening, not me! I vowed when you sent my boy up that I'd get you. Work kept me busy for a time — forging, if you'd like to know. Doesn't that make your hair curl? As soon as I'd cleaned up enough dough, I stepped out and got on your track. I fixed myself at a small place outside this village. I made myself nice and popular with all and sundry — including Sheriff Ingleby. I took the name of Grant and everybody thinks I'm a retired businessman. All so I could be near you. Swell set-up, eh?'

'So you are Amos Grant,' Langton breathed. 'I've heard of you.'

'I've waited my chance,' Gell went on. 'I studied your place here. I figured the best way to get in, the shape of the windows, everything. I knew when you'd be here. I knew even when you'd be alone . . . ' He stopped for a moment and smiled crookedly. 'I'm going to kill you, Langton,' he said gently.

'And go straight to executioner?' Langton parried, fighting for time. He was in a tight spot and knew it.

'No, not the executioner. This job is foolproof. See?'

Langton's eyes strayed back to his revolver drawer, but Gell's automatic still pointed unwaveringly. Langton forced an apparent calm.

'Gell, you're a damned fool! My son and his wife are coming here later on this evening from Chicago. If you kill me, they'll find my body before you have a chance to — '

'They are, eh?' Gell's eyes gleamed briefly. 'Good. Fits in nicely with my plan — '

He broke off as with a sudden lightning movement, Langton's right hand whipped up the heavy law book he'd been reading. In one hurtling movement he flung it unerringly at Gell's hand, spinning the automatic out of his clutch.

Langton dived, snatched at the desk drawer and tore it open. He was too vigorous — the draw came right out and flung its contents across the carpet. Before he could leap Gell had recovered his automatic and stood poised and ready.

'Better take it easy,' he advised coolly. 'Thanks for doing that. Your own gun will make it simpler . . . '

He picked it up warily in his handkerchief, jerked it open and glanced at the loaded chambers. He put his own gun away, slipped on a glove, held Langton's revolver steadily.

'Wait a minute — !' Langton shouted hoarsely, but at that identical moment, Gell fired.

The bullet struck clean into Langton's forehead, left a powder mark from the nearness of the fire. A welling trickle of blood went down his ashy, startled face. For a split second he remained standing there motionless — then he dropped heavily to the carpet.

Abruptly Gell was transformed into a man of action. Tearing off his wet hat and mackintosh, he hung them on the fireplace so they dripped to the warm hearth. Then he removed his solitary glove and substituted rubber gloves on both hands, flexed his fingers for a moment.

Working at top speed he commenced a systematic search of the desk, using Langton's own keys. At last he found the material he needed — a bundle of old letters and notes in Langton's own handwriting, together with a fountain pen. To Gell, a man whose very existence depended on his brilliancy as a forger, the next part of the scheme was comparatively simple.

Snatching notepaper he made several scrawls, then began a complete letter. In it he stated briefly that responsibilities, known and unknown, had driven Langton to suicide. The letter was skillfully signed, 'Rufus Langton'.

Gell read it through, nodded, sealed it in an envelope and penned the superscription — 'To Whom It May Concern.' He left it conspicuously on the desk

Then he put the keys back in Langton's pocket, hauled him into the chair by the desk, slumped him in the correct position. The revolver he put on the desk close to the outflung right hand. No slip-ups there, either: Langton had been right-handed all right.

Gell surveyed the result, then looked closely at the carpet for some sign of bloodstain. There was none; he had moved Langton in time . . . He turned to the fountain pen, but in his urgency to fix it in Langton's fingers, he nearly overlooked the contradictory aspect.

'Can't be,' he muttered. 'He wouldn't shoot, and *then* write . . . '

He whipped the pen away, cursed as it fell out of his hand. He turned, looking for it on the floor, trod on it. When he raised it, the nib was cross-legged.

For a moment he was nonplussed. No other pen on the desk: no nibs either, far as he could see. Then his eye caught the glint of a gold clasp on Langton's breast pocket. In an instant he had whipped out a fountain pen and unscrewed the cap. Nib was fairly similar: he could take that chance. He laid it down carefully, suggestively. Not likely this would be a murder problem anyway. He had laid his plan too well for that.

He made a final search, bundled the specimen forgery notes he had made into his pocket, along with the broken pen. The rest was a simple job. He removed all traces of wet from the polished woodwork near the window with his handkerchief, took his nearly dried coat and hat and donned them again, holding up the hems of the mackintosh so no stray drops could sprinkle. Then he retreated backwards out of the room, using the door this time. As he went, he removed all traces of mud he might have left behind.

The front door automatically latched itself behind him as he passed outside.

Immediately the full tearing fury of the wind and rain smote him. Long before he had completed the short journey along the rough shale pathway to his coupe, concealed in the main village road just outside the gates, he was struggling for breath and soddened with the downpour. All to the good, anyway, this weather; wash away all possible signs of footprints.

The moment he had slipped in the

driving seat he slammed in the first gear; soon he was streaking hell for leather down the road. Rain swilled in cascades down the windshield, blurring the vision of half-flooded road ahead. Wind twisted the steering wheel like a live thing in his fingers. He went on at desperate speed, following the only road into Railsby Bend village itself, a distance of perhaps five miles from the Judge's lodge.

The village loomed up at last, sepulchrally dark and gale-swept. Gell's car swished through the puddles of the empty high street, with its dim wavering lamps and rain-glistened houses, lights shining dully behind window shades.

He went on until he came to Sheriff Ingleby's office: then he jammed the brakes and came to a skidding standstill. Leaping from the car he dived for the warm, lighted interior of the place.

Sheriff Ingleby, thin and angular, with a bald head fringed with white fluff, was sitting reading beside the glowing iron stove, pipe in mouth, glasses on nose. He looked up in surprise over his lenses at Gell's sudden wet and spattering entry.

'Why, Mr. Grant! I sure didn't expect to see anybody around here tonight — certainly not you. Anythin' I can do?'

Gell smiled cordially enough under his dripping hat. So far, his plan was working perfectly. Five miles in seven minutes wasn't bad going on such a night. Then his eyes moved from the Sheriff's clock.

'Guess you wouldn't be seeing me now, Sheriff, only I'm nearly out of gas another seven miles to cover to get home. The filling station's too far off, even if it's open — which I doubt. I've just come from Chicago, and believe me it's been one lousy trip!'

'Yeah, I can imagine,' Ingleby sympathized. He rose stiffly to his feet, and slipped into huge oilskins.

'If I remember right, I've a gallon of gas over in the garage I can let you have. Be right back.'

Gell nodded and moved to the warmth of the stove. As he stood there, his mind clarified the last details. The Chicago alibi was foolproof, too: Jed Gunther, big businessman on the surface, racketeer deep down, had promised to provide the necessary verification that Gell had been in Chicago. Of course, a little forging job would be required as payment, but then —

Suddenly Ingleby was back with a can of gasoline in his hand.

'I reckon there's only half a gallon, but you can have it,' was his comment. 'I guess you — ' He glanced round in irritated surprise as the telephone bell sharply interrupted him. Grumbling he moved across to the instrument. 'Hope no guy has gotten himself into a mess on a night like this . . . '

Gell took the can and moved to the doorway. As he stood re-buttoning his mackintosh, Ingleby's words floated to him in snatches —

'Can't get through you say . . . ? Huh? Yeah, sure I understand . . . Okay, I'll see he gets to know, but I wished you'd picked a better night . . . What? Sure, I'll do it right now.'

Gell waited for no more. He was down the steps, fiddling with his tank, bracing himself against the lashing wind and rain. By the time he had added the spirit to the already half-full tank he was aware that Sheriff Ingleby was near him, pulling back the doors of his garage.

'Nice dam' job to send a man out on!' he complained, as Gell casually inquired the trouble. 'Serves me right for being generous. No need to do it — but I likes to give service . . . '

'Of course,' Gell said, handing over the empty tin and the money.

'Message to deliver — Judge Langton's place,' Ingleby growled. 'A good five miles from here, I guess.'

He turned away with that, climbed into his own car. Gell hesitated over asking more, then he decided otherwise. The nature of the message did not matter: what *did* matter was that luck was favouring him. Beyond doubt, Ingleby would find the suicide, and the short lapse of time would serve to strengthen the alibi.

Grinning to himself, Gell climbed back into his coupe, started off again into the raging storm.

Fifteen minutes later, Gell was home. His first action was to practically empty the car gas tank in case of a possible investigation, then the legitimacy of his call on the Sheriff could he proved. Oil he also drained plentifully. Generally he left the earmarks of a car that had covered a good distance and consumed plenty of fuel.

Then he went into the house, washed, changed into dry clothes, concealed his automatic, and afterwards repaired to the cosy warmth of his study dining room to eat a much-needed meal, and reflect on his scheme.

As he ate, the storm, if anything, seemed to increase in fury. The rain beat and splashed against the windows; the wind screamed in every nook and cranny. Momentary thoughts of flood from the River Kilvon, twenty miles distant, assailed his mind. If that happened, he might possibly be washed out by morning. It had happened once: it could happen again.

Then as he considered this unpleasant prospect he was abruptly startled by a hammering on the outer front door. A faint smile touched his hard lips. So

Sheriff Ingleby was on a trail of inquiry already, eh? Good!

He opened the door and registered mild astonishment as the dripping form of Ingleby trooped in. He pulled off his oilskins in a flurry of raindrops, then went across to the crackling fire.

'Well, I'm darned glad to be outa that stuff for a few minutes,' he declared with feeling. Never saw a night like it in years.'

Gell quietly agreed with him, proffered a drink that Ingleby consumed with slow satisfaction. Then he said:

'I'm here to bring a bit of a shock, Mr. Grant. You know Judge Langton, of course? Well, he's — committed suicide.'

'No!' Gell's exclamation came in a half whisper of amazed horror: it was just the right inflection. He gave a little puzzled shake of his head. 'Well, this is bad news, Sheriff! But — but when did it happen?' he asked curiously. 'I was talking to him only two days ago. I suppose it must have been recently, and you found it out tonight?'

Ingleby stood with his back to the fire, shook his head moodily.

'Y'see, I had a message for him: his telephone was out of order with the storm so the message was put through to me. You remember I started off for his place? When I arrived there, there was no answer. I waited a while, knowing he ought to be there somewhere, then as nothing happened, I became worried, and forced a way in. I found him dead at his desk with a suicide confession right in front of him. Shot himself in the head at close range. I left a man down there in charge and went in search of Doc Morgan. He figgered Langton shot himself around eight-thirty tonight.'

'Poor old Langton,' Gell sighed regretfully.

'Naturally I've to make a few inquiries as to his reasons for suicide. He just said 'responsibilities, known and unknown,' but that conveys nothin' . . . You say you talked to him two days ago?'

Gell nodded. 'I seem to remember he said something about feeling depressed, now I think of it. Tough work, being a Judge.'

'Yeah . . . ' Ingleby looked thoughtful.

'Did he make any particular statement that might hint at suicide?'

'Not that I recall.' Gell was frowning a little now, but still at his ease. What the devil was the old fool getting at, anyway?

Ingleby looked up suddenly from studying the rug. His lean face was grim.

'No, I'm danged sure you don't recall! Langton didn't commit suicide. He was murdered!'

'What!' Gell exclaimed, starting. 'But Sheriff, who on earth — '

'Keep right where you are, Grant — if that's your right name.' Ingleby's hand was closed now in his right pocket. There was a significant bulge there. 'I'm not joking,' he added, drawing the revolver to light. 'You're under arrest on suspicion of the murder of Langton.'

Gell could not help his gasp of surprise. 'Why — you're crazy! What the hell right have you to come in here and make an assertion like that? Why, I was with you at the approximate time of this — this murder! You must remember!'

'I remember,' Ingleby said curtly. 'But that don't make no difference to me. I'm going to book you! You figgered on a perfect alibi, knowing that it wouldn't be possible to reckon to a few minutes just when Langton died. But you tripped up on one or two things, Grant! You placed a fountain pen in Langton's hand with which he supposedly wrote his suicide confession . . .

'What happened to the original pen that wrote the note doesn't make much odds: what *does* make odds is the fact that the fountain pen had no ink in it! The barrel was dry as a bone and the rubber tube had a hole in it. Langton musta worn it for an ornament.'

The sudden flaw took Gell off his guard. He began to bluster, but Ingleby cut him short.

'An' there were other things! Scratches on the window-catch, a spot or two of mud from outside, on the carpet, one or two raindrops still slightly wet on the blotting pad . . . '

Gell flamed, 'Damn you, man, flimsy evidence like this isn't going to get you any place! Where's the motive? Anybody might have done it. I couldn't have done it, I tell you! I was driving from Chicago all this evening until I got to your office. Ring up, and find out!'

'I reckon I don't need to do that,' Ingleby replied grimly. 'You say you didn't stop until you got to my place?'

'Right!'

Ingleby seemed to reflect for a moment. 'S'pose you know Langton was expecting his son and daughter-in-law tonight, from Chicago?'

'How should I know?' Gell snarled.

'I just thought you might. It was the son who telephoned me at my office — he and his wife are stranded outside Railsby Bend. They wanted me to tell the Judge they couldn't make it.'

'So what?' Gell snapped.

'So this! You say you didn't stop any place. What time did you cross the Kilvon River Bridge?'

Gell gestured impatiently. 'How should I know exactly? About half an hour before I reached your place, I suppose. Couldn't have been more.'

'That's what I reckoned,' Ingleby said, smiling bleakly. 'A distance of fifteen miles. But the point is that Langton's son also told me that the bridge had been washed away two hours before you got to my place! Yet you didn't stop anywhere! By no possible means could a car have gotten across the river into Railsby Bend tonight! It only struck me later when I remembered you saying you'd come from Chicago.' The Sheriff stopped, his lips taut.

'Better get your things. Grant. You've some explaining to do! And hurry up!'

3

BEAST OF THE TARN

Revil Draycott had never really liked the cat, anyhow. It was too clever, too intelligent, and seemed to hurl constant reminders at him of the time when he had slain his wife and thrown her body into the bottomless depths of Gilpin's Tarn. She had died with the vow that her cat would avenge her when it, too, died. Strange sort of statement — probably the empty vapourings of the dying.

Just the same, Draycott did not like the cat. It followed him everywhere, in the fields or sheds as he went about his farming work; sat by him as he milked the cows, took up a position directly opposite him whenever he had a meal.

There was something uncanny about its devotion to him, and a strange fire was always kindling in its big great eyes as though it knew his secret and waited only for a chance to rake him with vicious claws.

In appearance it was not a particularly unusual animal — merely one of the tabby varieties with a bushy tail and solid bullet head. Only its eyes were different — big, hypnotic, accusing.

Draycott tolerated its presence for nearly two years after the carefully planned 'disappearance' of his wife, only hesitating to kill it because of the vow she had made. But there came a time when he was goaded into action — when the creature, in snatching a trifling morsel of food from him, dug its sharp claws into his brown hand,

Instantly he leaped up from the table, scowling down on the blood oozing from the scratches. His cruel grey eyes shot to the cat as it scuttled away from him.

'You blasted little green-eyed devil!' he burst out furiously. 'What the devil did you do that for? By heaven, I'll show you what I do with brutes like you!'

The cat slunk further away, tail down and eyes gleaming. But it did not slink far. Stooping, Draycott seized it by the scruff of the neck and, holding it at arm's length, walked across the farmyard to the neighbouring barn. Once there he dropped the animal inside a sack and closed the neck, oblivious to the creature's wail of fright.

His tea forgotten in his smouldering anger, Draycott slung the bag over his shoulder and marched outside, through the farmyard and to the meadows beyond. He continued steadily onward toward the winter sunset, ignoring the threshing burden he clutched so immovably. His mind was focused on one spot, which he had not visited for two years: Gilpin's Tarn, about a mile and a half from his farm, just outside the village of Little Benton. Once in those bottomless waters the cat would worry him no more — would disappear as completely as his wife had done.

He gained the place at length and dropped the sack. The mewing from within fell unheeded upon his ears as he stood looking over the quietness to the lights of the village, and beyond them to the horizon bulk of Michigan. All was quiet save for the faint medley of sounds from the distant circus sideshows, at

77

Little Benton on one of its periodic visits. Yes, everything was quite deserted.

His gaze dropped presently to the black waters of the tarn itself, lying at the bottom of the craggy hundred-foot drop. Some said that the tarn had once been a mine; still others averred that it went straight down into the maw of hell. Idle village gossip, of course, but nonetheless here was an excellent place in which to throw bodies that must leave no trace.

Draycott hesitated for the briefest instant, suddenly recalling the vow of his wife. If he killed the cat —

With an impatient shrug he stooped, and picked up a small boulder, fastened it securely to the bag neck. Then seizing the entire bulk in his hands, he flung it far out into space, watched the stone jerk downward and plunge into the midst of those scummy, evil depths. The bag vanished in an eddy of frothing bubbles.

He stood grinning and looking down, squatting on his heels and waiting until the bubbling ceased and the tarn became placid again. It was nearly dark when he stood up. Everything was still quiet, and a threat of impending rain hung in the heavy air. An evil miasma was rising from the somber waters below. With the slightest of shudders, stricken suddenly by a peculiar fear of the calmness, Draycott turned and retraced his way home.

Yet at every step he took, he could mentally see the cat; see its eyes regarding him in the swirling wraiths of mist rising from the wet ground, could hear as though afar off its plaintive mewing.

'Nasty, rotten little beast,' he muttered thickly, rubbing his unshaven chin reminiscently. 'About as bad as its mistress. Funny to think how they both went down in the tarn.' He brooded over that and in a vicious, vengeful frame of mind finally gained the farm once more.

That night he slept badly, and was glad to get up in the coldness of the very early morning and prepare for his small milk round. For a reason he could not fathom, he found it impossible to rid himself altogether of the memory of that animal.

It had gone down so swiftly, so silently. Just that little vortex of bubbles. Just like his wife had done, helpless, never to be found again. No body — no proof. That had been clever! Now she was with her beloved cat again on the other side of eternity —

Draycott surprised himself standing with his mouth gaping, pursuing his reflections. With a start he realized how far his conscience had taken him back along the road of murder and hate. Pulling himself together, he forced himself to attend to his work and prepared for the morning round.

Things seemed different that morning. Everybody he met seemed apart from his own troubles. By the time he arrived home again in the late evening, a somber and heavy gloom had descended upon him. He was alone; his two cowhands had left for the day. In morose silence he prepared his solitary meal.

As he slowly ate by the light of the oil lamp, his eyes settled on the shadowy spot where the cat had always squatted at mealtimes. In his mind's eye he could again see those big, silently accusing eyes, the only eyes that had seen him murder his wife and drag her out in the dead of night to the tarn. The animal had followed at his heels, been the only silent witness to the crime. He reflected that he would have drowned it there and then had it not been for his wife's dying threat.

Well, what of it? He smiled twistedly. The cat was dead now, and no harm had come to him. Obviously her words had been the ravings of one on the edge of eternity.

Just the same, it mightn't do any harm to have a look at the tarn and reassure himself. He couldn't altogether feel too sure that all was well there.

'Chasin' a crazy idea, I guess,' was his growling comment, as he rose and lighted a storm lantern. 'About time I took myself in hand, instead of behavin' like a durned fool.'

He slipped into his oilskins, seized the lamp and went outside. Soft drizzling rain was falling, making the ground of the fields beyond the farm sodden and mushy. He progressed deliberately, alone in a world of cold and dankness. His emotions dropped to zero. Jaw outthrust, eyes staring ahead, he clumped steadily in the tarn's direction.

Finally he gained it. Setting down his lamp on a ledge of rock, he stared reflectively into the stenching stagnation below. A low sigh of relief escaped him at seeing nothing different. His inner expectations of some supernatural manifestation were unrealized.

He turned to go at length, satisfied — then abruptly stopped. The storm lantern nearly fell from his hands with fright, and his goggling eyes fixed themselves on the mushy, ill-defined path at his feet. For there, clearly imprinted, were the marks of an animal's foot. A large foot, too, complete with claws, heading away from the tarn.

Draycott had no idea how long he was held transfixed by that unexpected sight. It held his body and soul with its spell, but at last his eyes jerked from the imprints to the tarn again. A quivering hand pulled shudderingly at his lower lip.

'No — no, it can't be!' he shouted hoarsely. 'You couldn't have gotten out of that tarn! You couldn't!'

He fell silent again, shaking so violently that he had to rest for a moment against a nearby rock. The oppressive quiet hemmed him in. His scared, disordered mind painted that quiet with all manner of incredible fantasies. He could have sworn that he heard the voice of his wife, thin and far distant, rising from those murky depths — accusing him, laughing at him, triumphant in the knowledge that her beloved cat was abroad in the dark waiting to spring, to exact a tearing, snapping vengeance for the brutal thing he had done.

Weak from strain, he forced himself up at last and staggered shakily along the path. Immediately he left it, the tracks of those feline feet vanished in the crushed and rain-sodden grass of the moorland. Fright was cramping him now. He went forward at a half run, convinced that some shadowy terror was waiting to emerge from the tarn and seize him.

It was then, as he ran, that he became conscious of something else. Not an echo of his own sogging, sloughing footfalls, but a deliberate and steady padding in the gloom some little distance behind him. When he stopped the sound stopped too, and left him alone in that horrible, dank emptiness.

He twisted a fearful face toward the dark behind him, but saw nothing. He went on again, more slowly, not looking where he was going — and suddenly found himself flat on his face in the mud with the storm lantern dashed out beside him.

'Who's — who's there?' he screamed hoarsely, as he scrambled up again. 'Why are you following me like this? Who are you?'

There was no response save the croak of a bullfrog at his feet, sending his heart slamming harder than ever For a full minute he stood gaping into the drenching, obscuring mist, then there came to his ears a low and chilling whine like the cry of a whipped puppy. Instantly his mind flashed back to the plaintive cry the cat had given when he'd pushed it in the sack.

'You!' he shouted hoarsely. 'You're out of the tarn — dead! You're three times your size! Waiting there in the dark — '

He twirled back again and commenced to run blindly through the abyss, heart bumping against his side until he thought it would fail him and drop him into eternity. The padding feet were swifter now, bounding after him, carrying something he couldn't see but which his anguished mind knew was some gargantuan reincarnation of the helpless animal he had drowned. The warning of his dead wife was coming true —

By the time he reached his cottage he was in a pitiable state. Mud-smothered and drenched in rain and sweat, hand shaking so much he could hardly raise the door latch. He stumbled blindly within and fumbled with matches — stood shivering violently as the yellow flame kindled into an amber glow.

Silence grouped around the farm now — heavy, suggestive silence that had a portent of impending disaster. Draycott found himself moving about on tiptoe, afraid to disturb the quiet. His oilskins rustled unnervingly as he tugged them off amidst a shower of raindrops.

Then he moved to the fireplace and tried to coax the smouldering embers into some semblance of life. Failing, he sat by the darkened grate in the deep shadows and tried to compose himself.

His mind was on fire now. Memories of his wife and the cat pulsated alternately through his brain. The tarn, the prints of the enlarged cat, the wail in the mist, the soft footfalls that had followed him back — they were all gigantically magnified in his brain, sent gelid stiffness into his joints and nerves.

Suddenly he stiffened. That wailing again! It reached him clearly from the silence outside, the wail of an angry, lonely beast. Trembling he rose up and snatched down a rifle from the wall, though even as he did so he knew it would be useless against something reincarnated from death itself.

Step by step, shaking with each movement, he went to the window and pulled aside the faded curtains. What he saw was an actual physical as well as mental shock. Dimly visible in the reflected light from the swinging oil lamp was the face of the drowned cat, incredibly huge and ferocious, fur plastered wetly to its head just as it had emerged from those water logged depths.

Dazed, weakened with horror, Draycott's terrified eyes fixed their gaze upon the horrible fanged teeth, upper lip drawn back in a hideous snarl of vengeful cruelty.

Then the eyes — brazen, malevolent orbs boring from the midst of that frame of sodden fur. Blazing green, catching the light — Draycott fell backwards, overpowered with the shock, and groped weakly for the table for support.

After a while he steadied himself and slammed over the huge bar of wood that bolted the door, tremblingly clutched his gun once more as there came a fiendish scratching and tearing at the woodwork, accompanied by a throaty growling and snarling.

'You can't come back!' Draycott screamed madly. 'Evelyn, my wife, if you are anywhere within hearing, call off this terrible cat! I can stand anything but this monstrous reincarnation of the creature I destroyed! Please — please, I beg of you! You were right in saying that the cat's death would avenge you! I admit it! Take it away!'

As though in response to his sobbing entreaty silence fell again. There were no sounds from outside. Little by little Draycott began to recover himself, gradually convinced himself that somewhere in the unknown his long-dead wife had heard him and recalled the hideous reincarnation back to the mystic hell from which it had emerged.

He relaxed a little and cautiously lifted the heavy wooden bar from the door — opened it very gently. But the instant he did so something vomited from the dark outside to the accompaniment of a piercing, paralyzing shriek. A vast body, terrible claws outspread, hurtled inwards and struck Draycott clean in the chest, sending him hurtling backwards helplessly.

'Evelyn!' he yelled madly, struggling frantically. 'Evelyn! Call off this cat of yours! Call off this cat — !'

Then his words froze as his arms

stiffened helplessly, powerless to ward off that fanged abyss of death closing in upon him —

The following day the *Little Benton Times* carried a report that was brief but significant. It read:

Mr. Revil Draycott, well-known farmer of Little Benton, met his death last night in tragic circumstances. All day yesterday a tiger, escaped from the Little Benton circus, was being searched for unsuccessfully, owing to the mist. Its trail was finally picked up at Gilpin's Tarn and the animal itself was found at Mr. Draycott's farm. Unfortunately Mr. Draycott was evidently killed in trying to attack the tiger, which had obviously been attracted to the farm by the livestock.

The tiger is now back in the circus and Mr. Draycott's death will be much regretted by those who knew him.

4

SAFETY IN NUMBERS

When Andrew Denham first saw the letter lying open on the bureau in Evelyn Carstairs' flat he felt that it was confirmation of all the suspicions he had developed in the four months he had been engaged to the girl. There was nothing definitely wrong, of course — no visible sign that another man had come into her life, but — Anyway, the letter was there, open for anybody to read.

Ethically, Andrew had no right to look at the letter at all, but being on familiar terms in Evelyn's flat he stood looking at it as he waited for her to finish dressing for their theatre date. He hesitated, asked his conscience a couple of questions, then picked the letter up and read it —

Thursday

Dearest Evelyn,
I shall be looking forward to our little

meeting as arranged. I have something awfully important to ask you. With all my love,
   Ernie.

Andrew put the letter down slowly and scowled.

'No address even,' he muttered. 'Must be on very intimate terms, especially to add 'with all my love' . . . '

He looked about the comfortable room as though expecting to see some signs of Ernie, but there were none. Only that adoring letter left on the bureau so blatantly —

Then Evelyn came bustling out of the bedroom, exquisitely gowned, drawing a fur cape about her shoulders. Andrew studied her absently — the sheen of her blonde hair, the delicately applied make-up on her face. She was definitely a good-looking girl, with a figure as perfect as her vocation of salon mannequin demanded.

'Well, well, Andy, why so serious?' she enquired, smiling. 'We're going to the theatre, not the dentist's, remember!'

He gave a start. His darkly handsome face broke into a forced smile.

'Sorry. Just something I was thinking about . . . Come along.'

He opened the door for her, then he hesitated outside.

'Got your key? Since you say you've only one you'd better make sure.'

She looked in her handbag and while she did so he idly studied the door with its bulbous-curled numbers — 129. Two screws in each number, and even they seemed too many. He found himself thinking what trifling details one notices sometimes when waiting —

'Yes, I have it,' Evelyn said after a moment, and with a nod he pulled the door shut.

Four doors further along the lengthy, softly-carpeted corridor there were voices raised high in anger — a man's and a woman's.

'All right, all right, if that's how you feel about it!' the woman's voice was shouting. 'I'm sick and tired of you and that's the truth! And don't slam the door as you go out. The screws on the numbers are coming out already — !'

'Nice people you live amongst,' Andrew murmured, as the girl and he stood side by side in the self-service lift on its journey to the ground floor.

She shrugged. 'There have been quite a few complaints about Mr. and Mrs. Baxter in 126. They fight like cat and dog. It's high time the management did something. Thank heavens I'm four doors removed from them — but I honestly think the tenants of all the flats on that floor must hear the rows.'

The lift came to a stop. Andrew pushed back the grille-gates and followed the girl out to the taxi he had ordered. He said nothing during journey to the theatre, and even when they got there he remained with his lips firm, looking at the gleam of the satin-faced curtains across the stage

'Is anything the matter, Andy?' Evelyn asked at length. 'You seem to have very little to say for yourself.'

'This isn't perhaps the time to say what I'm thinking — just before the show starts,' he said; 'but tell me something!

What's come between us during the last few weeks?'

'*Between* us?' she repeated, surprised.

'Oh, I know it's nothing obvious — nothing you can nail down as an absolute fact, but I've had the feeling that . . . Well, that perhaps I'm not the all-in-all fiance I used to be.'

'But, Andy, how absurd! Whatever gave you that idea?'

'For one thing you cancelled three of our evening dates on the run, and gave no logical explanation; for another you asked that the date of our wedding be postponed indefinitely — '

'But Andy, I *told* you — purely for business reasons!'

'For business reasons, eh? And I was mug enough to believe it — then! Suppose you tell me who *Ernie* is?'

Evelyn stared at the challenging dark eyes. She seemed about to answer when the orchestra struck up the overture. She had to wait for a moment or two and during that time a change of expression came to her face. Her mouth hardened and her eyes lost their light of cheerful interest.

'How do you know so much about Ernie?' she asked briefly, during a quieter piece in the music. 'From that letter I left on the bureau?'

'Exactly — that dear loving letter! He has something 'awfully important to ask you' and he signs himself 'With all my love' — That explains everything! the reason for cancelling our dates, the reason for postponing our wedding . . . Business reasons indeed! He's somebody else you've taken on, isn't he? I'm just a nuisance and you want to be rid of me!'

The girl was silent as the music thundered. She was obviously thinking hard. Then she said coldly:

'I always had the feeling that you were the suspicious, insanely jealous type, Andy, and now I'm sure of it. When you'll even descend to reading my correspondence . . . ' She got to her feet suddenly and looked down at him. 'Allow me to pass, please.'

'But — but what about the show?'

'I prefer not to see it, thank you!'

Andrew got up awkwardly. He could not make a scene there and then with the audience packed in around him and casting curious glances. Muttering under his breath he followed the girl up the gangway and caught her arm as they entered the foyer.

'Look here, Evelyn, at least explain yourself — !'

'Explain *myself* indeed!' Her grey eyes blazed scorn at him. 'It seems to me that that's all on your side — Let go of my arm, and don't ever speak to me again!'

She tugged herself free and he stood watching her stalking sway amongst the late theatre-comers. He did not attempt to follow her. Lighting a cigarette, he stood thinking.

'Probably just what she wanted, anyway,' he muttered finally. 'A clear chance to break with me — and did she seize it!'

He turned aside and went into the bar, spent perhaps half an hour consuming drinks more for the sake of something to do than aught else. As he drank, his suspicions deepened, reformed, and took on divers shapes.

She *had* cancelled three evening dates in a row — What other reason than for another man — for Ernie? Couldn't be because of her work when the salon closed at 5.30. And she *had* said they must postpone their wedding for a while. Business reasons! The only reason was that she wanted to be rid of him before the walk to the altar. The whole thing was now perfectly clear.

And how — Ernie! Evelyn had made a fatal mistake in leaving that letter lying about, unless she had been femininely clever and had left it on purpose to build up to the final break.

'Women!' Andrew muttered, staring at his empty glass. 'Tricky as cats! Give 'em half a chance and they'll get their claws into you — But who does she think she is to treat *me* like this?'

He got to his feet, swayed a little, and stared round the smoke-hazed saloon. He suddenly realized that he had taken it all lying down. She had treated him like a tiresome schoolboy — It had not seemed to matter much then, but it did now. The number of drinks he had consumed insisted that he demand an explanation.

Unsteadily he left the bar, went

through the foyer and to the outdoors. The fresh air cleared his head somewhat. He began to walk briskly, arrived at the big building containing Evelyn's flat some fifteen minutes later.

Sullenly he walked across to the service lift, had some difficulty in dragging over the grille-gates and finding the right button — then he pressed it and glided slowly up the shaft. He was nearing the top when the blur in his mind was pierced by a woman's voice —

'Good bye, Ernie — best of luck!'

Andrew started and dragged himself erect. He wished his head were not quite so confused, that he had been listening properly to the voice, But *Ernie* — ?

His eyes narrowed as the lift came to a halt at the floor he wanted. A big, broad-shouldered man, well dressed and in the early thirties was standing waiting for it. He gave Andrew a glance and stepped into the lift, then as Andrew remained standing looking at him he made a motion.

'Going down, sir?' he enquired.

Andrew drew the grille into place and

fumbled for the 'Ground Floor' button.

'Yes,' he whispered. 'I'm going down . . . with you!'

'Oh! Well, that's all right, then.'

'So you think it's all right, do you?' Andrew's voice was still low; then he suddenly stabbed at the 'Stop' button and brought the lift to a halt between floors. He gave a crooked smile.

'What in thunder's the matter with you?' the man demanded. 'Are you drunk, or what?'

'You're Ernie, aren't you?' Andrew asked bitterly; then as the other nodded in vague surprise Andrew added, 'We're in just the right place to thrash this out! The lift's stopped between floors and nobody can open the gates or reach us until we get to a floor-level again . . . So you are Ernie!'

The man looked at him for a long moment, his eyes narrowing.

'Yes, I'm Ernie — and I know who you are too! You're the man who's been in my way! Well, I'm glad to have seen you, anyway — ' He tugged out a Yale key and held it up between finger and thumb.

'You see? I'm the one who's going to do the talking from now on!'

He broke off as Andrew suddenly lashed out with his fist. It took Ernie on the side of the jaw and sent him reeling against the wall. Simultaneously he caught the back of his head on the button-box control, gasped, then slumped weakly to the floor.

Andrew stood glaring down on him, his lips compressed — then with sudden savagery he snatched the key up from where it had fallen from the man's hand.

'Even got the key to her flat, eh? And the only key, too! More than I ever got! I'll show that two-timing little she-cat!'

Andrew paused, staring at the inside coat pocket of the man. The lapel had fallen aside to reveal the butt of a revolver, sheathed in cellophane. For a moment Andrew hesitated, then he snatched the gun out, tore away the cellophane, and found it was a .32. Funny for a private citizen to be carrying a gun . . . must be a reason.

He was too reckless, too inwardly worked up with fury and drinks to care much what he did. He snatched out the man's wallet and went through it quickly. Practically the first thing he encountered was a warrant-card which read — 'Criminal Investigation Department. Metropolitan Police. Name, Ernest Billings. Rank, Detective-Sergeant. First Class. Height 5ft 10 ins. Hair black. No distinguishing marks.'

A Detective-Sergeant, of all people! Then why the gun? Andrew knew enough of law to realize that an off-duty English policeman would not normally be carrying firearms —

It didn't signify. What *did* signify was that Evelyn had obviously transferred her affections to him, that she had called 'Good bye' to him, and therefore must be at home — and here was a gun! Things seemed to link up in Andrew' a mind. Half mechanically he broke the gun-magazine and looked at it. Two spent cartridges were ejected. Four other bullets remained intact, unfired.

He made up his mind. He sent the lift down to the ground floor and looked anxiously into the entrance hall. There was nobody in sight at the moment. Opening the grille he dragged the unconscious man out and dumped him outside the gateway — then he returned into the lift and sent it upwards again.

His pulses throbbing and his feet unsteady he walked out into the corridor, leaving the grille-gate wide open. The hangover from the drink was blurring his vision a little. It seemed to be upsetting his conception of distance too. He had always thought it was further along the corridor to Evelyn's flat — only it wasn't. Right here before him was 129.

He glanced about him once and then tried the key. It fitted exactly, and being a Yale that meant it had to be Evelyn's flat. Softly he turned the key and entered the dimly lighted room beyond. There was only a reading lamp, shining on a blonde head, just visible over the top of the divan. Andrew knew the sheen of that lovely hair.

He stared at it malevolently, wondering why Evelyn had pulled the divan round to the fire instead of leaving it in its usual position by the wall — then he gripped the revolver tightly and fired — four times — straight at the head before him.

It vanished. There was a thud as the woman's body fell to the floor.

'If you don't want me you'll certainly not get Ernie,' he muttered; then he backed uncertainly out of the room and closed the door, stood breathing hard and gripping the knob on the outside.

As though from far away he was conscious of the sound of feet plodding up the rubberoid stairs. In fact there were two pairs of feet — He turned stupidly to look. It was quite impossible, of course, but there, supporting the dazed but now fully conscious Detective-Sergeant Billings, stood Evelyn, still with the fur wrap about her shoulders, her expression a mixture between puzzlement and anger.

'Are you all right now?' she asked the Detective-Sergeant.

'Yes, miss — and thanks for your help.' Billings looked at the gaping Andrew. 'If you'd have shut the gates, sir, this young lady wouldn't have needed to help me upstairs. We could have used the lift ... And I'll take that gun if you don't mind! *And* you might explain why you hit me in the jaw!'

Andrew stared at him. 'Gun?' he repeated absently.

'The one in your hand . . . And you've messed it up beautifully, I see! I had it in a cellophane envelope to preserve finger-prints. It belongs to a case on which I'm working . . . '

Andrew handed it over mechanically, his eyes moving to Evelyn.

'Where — did you come from?' he whispered. 'I can understand you helping Ernie here, but — '

'Ernie?' Evelyn repeated blankly. 'But — but don't be absurd! When I came in after a walk round after that row we had I found the Sergeant in the entrance hall, holding his head. He said somebody had hit him and asked me to help him upstairs so he could see in this flat here . . . Now I find the man is you, of all people!'

'Then — this *isn't* Ernie — ?'

'My name's Ernest Billings,' the Yard man said, sniffing the gun. 'And this gun has been *fired*!' he added ominously. 'By

God, if you've shot your wife — !'

'Wife?' Evelyn repeated in bewilderment.

Billings raised his eyes to the Yale lock on the doorway. The key was still in it. Sudden alarm on his face he dashed into the flat and looked about him. When he came out again his face was grim and he clamped a hand on Andrew's arm.

'I think you'd better come along with me — '

'Andy, Andy, what have you done?' Evelyn demanded hoarsely.

'I dunno. I thought this was Ernie — '

'But not *my* Ernie!' Evelyn interrupted. ' 'Ernie' is simply the short for 'Ernestine.' She's my best friend. We go lots of places together. I'd have told you tonight only I thought you were so horribly suspicious I decided against it.'

'Oh!' Andrew licked his lips. 'And — and the nights you wouldn't keep our dates? The postponement of the wedding?'

'I *told* you — business reasons. On the nights I cancelled the dates I was at the salon trying on some new secret creations for export. I couldn't breathe a word about them. I postponed the wedding because of the possibility that I might be sent abroad to demonstrate . . . '

'I don't know what all this means, but I *do* know you've shot Mildred Baxter dead!' Billings said grimly. 'I see the mistake now. I mistook you for her husband when you seemed to know all about me. I was in love with her and her husband was making her life a hell. I called in here tonight on my way to headquarters to ask how she was getting on with divorce arrangements — '

'But you had the key to Evelyn's flat!' Andrew insisted. 'It's still in the door there!'

'My key's here,' Evelyn said quickly, pulling it out of her handbag.

'I had the key to *Mildred's* flat,' Billings stated. 'She gave me a spare one so I could see her at the times her husband was away. I've never seen him personally, of course — '

'But the number's 129! It says so!'

All three of them stared at it. There was no doubt about it — they glanced round at an interruption. A janitor wearing overalls was approaching along the corridor. As he came up he looked at the three in puzzlement. Then Billings pulled the door to hastily.

'Evening, folks,' the janitor greeted. 'Anythin' I c'n do?'

'Er — no,' Billings said.

The janitor shrugged, pulled a screwdriver out of his pocket and went to the door. Deliberately he turned the '9' round to its normal position of '6' and screwed it tight.

'Worst of these darned numbers,' he growled. 'Only two screws in each of 'em, and not very good screws at that. Always coming out. Same as here now — One screw loose, left in the top of the loop, workin' like a central pivot as you might say. The top screw comes out of the tail and the heavy loop on the tail makes the number turn right over . . . I should ha' fixed it earlier. Mrs. Carter rang down this morning and said the door numbers screws were comin' loose. Must be through slammin' the door too hard . . . '

The janitor sighed and put his screwdriver back in his pocket.

'Well, that's that. Never do to 'ave two rooms with the same number. Might be mix-ups, eh?'

Andrew stared after the janitor as he went off whistling.

'Might be!' he whispered. 'My God, if only you knew!'

5

GLASS NEMESIS

I arrived in New York's Hotel Europa in a crate with straw wrapped around me. Once I was yanked into the daylight I took my place amidst hundreds of other short, transparent cylinders like myself.

Then, after a period of being filled with all manner of spirits, after being caressed by the lips of men and women alike, I found myself in Room 402 on the third floor.

One evening, about nine o'clock, a man and woman came in, both in evening dress. I liked the look of the woman; she was young and pretty — but the man was a grim piece of work. Lean face, dark, with a voice like caustic soda.

Anyhow they got around to talking. I figured they were husband and wife. As the man talked he picked me and my fellow up from the tray and started to pour spirit into both of us. But he did something kind of different to me.

Turning a little, he poured powder into me and handed me over to the girl.

Her hand closed around me. She drank my contents and relaxed in the armchair. The man started talking again.

'There's only one thing to do with people like you, Mary, and I've done it! Since you won't give me grounds for divorce, I've made my own grounds. I'll marry Claire Blake in spite of you!'

The woman's voice was low and bitter. 'You know, Barry, you are a rotten beast! The rottenest I've ever known! What's more, I'm going to put Claire Blake wise to the fact before you start in to two-time her, as you have me . . . You're only after her seven million dollars, so you may as well admit it. 'That's why you want to be rid of me!'

She stopped talking and put me back on the tray. Picking me up, Barry started to polish my outside with a handkerchief. When he was through he polished my companion both inside and out and left it as clean as a new window.

'Turning waiter?' questioned the woman, laconically.

'No, my dear. Just a little preparation, that's all . . . I'm meeting Claire tonight at the West Fork Road-house at ten o'clock. That gives me very little time to finish things off here first . . . '

He put his handkerchief in his pocket and studied the cloying dregs in my base.

Suddenly the woman tried to get to her feet, but she fell back. Holding her white throat, she shouted, hoarsely:

'Barry! Barry, what have you done to me? I'm — I'm choking — '

'That poison's pretty fast,' he answered, and his voice, reminded me of steel blades rubbing together. 'I've polished my own glass inside and out and your glass on the outside only. That leaves it clear for this . . . ' Taking her quivering hand he clamped her fingers around me, then let her go. Grinning viciously, he said: 'Evidence for suicide, my dear . . . '

The woman just couldn't do anything but gasp and gulp hoarsely. Barry went out and locked the door from the outside . . . For a moment nothing happened, then driven by the frantic urge for air, for relief, the woman suddenly writhed out of the chair and dropped to her knees.

She tried to reach the window, but just couldn't make it. Instead she clutched hold of me and hurled me base-foremost at the window, breaking the glass. Her weak, strangled cry of 'Help! Air!' followed me — then I thudded down on leather.

I didn't break. I'm pretty tough. I was in the car park back of the hotel. The car park attendant was bawling a little distance off.

Then his voice came close to the open two-seater in which I'd landed. Silks started rustling and suddenly a smartly dressed young woman clambered into the driving-seat beside me. Since it was pretty dark she didn't see me, of course. Pursing up her painted lips she started to whistle.

Something bounded out of the gloom and plumped almost on top of me. A dog of sorts: Great Dane, I think it was. A real hefty brute, anyway . . . The girl made him lie down, then had her bags fixed in the rumble seat. She looked at her watch, then started up the engine. The car went smoothly into the High Street and headed out of town at a spanking pace.

Now and again she looked at the dog and said: 'Take it easy, Kong; don't be so darned affectionate! I've got a wheel to look after.'

We were on the main country road, heading west when something sharp started pulling at me. It was Kong's hefty paw. He raked me over then thrust his huge, wet tongue in my insides, started licking and licking until he'd taken up all that sediment. Then I rolled into the corner and stopped there. The dame was doing sixty-five and kept looking at the dashboard clock.

'I'll only just make it for ten if I step on it,' she muttered, then she pressed her foot harder on the accelerator and sent the car screaming through the dark down that ribbon of country road.

All of a sudden Kong started to move uneasily. His paws kneaded up and down like engine pistons. He let out the most horrible wail, as though he'd heard music being played somewhere.

The girl looked at him momentarily, startled. Then she snapped out: 'Kong!

Sit down! Sit down — !'

Half her sentence was drowned out by the roar and hoot of a car trying to overtake not half a mile behind. It couldn't have been doing less than seventy.

Kong howled again and leapt up entreatingly. In trying to draw the girl's attention to himself he struck her in the face with his paw . . . She screamed wildly, jammed her feet down helplessly on clutch and brake pedals, then let go of the steering-wheel with the sudden shock.

The car slewed round giddily and went shooting diagonally across the road. The overtaking auto stood no chance — Steel, rubber, glass and leather compressed into a triangular hell of destruction. Bags initialed 'C. B.' vomited from the rumble seat . . .

I rolled out to the side of the road. Some time after the woman dragged herself free, blood running down her face, her clothes torn and ripped. She looked for her dog and couldn't find him.

Then she staggered across to where a figure lay in the road, the head bent at an unnatural angle. There was a pause filled with the crackling of flames, then she screamed frantically:

'Dead! Oh, God — ! *Barry!*'

6

THE WAILING HYBRID

1

The Living Heart

As he drove swiftly through the night Jeff Rowland's thoughts were pleasant indeed, as he dwelt with a certain schoolboyish satisfaction on the circus he had attended in Castleford village not an hour before. It represented his fourth successive visit.

Helen Vane had been there, of course, performing her usual magic and snake-charming act. There seemed to be no snake she could not handle, from a cobra to a boa. Helen — a delightful girl, appealing strongly to him by the very reason of her fearless cleverness. He thanked the fortune that had led him to see the first performance — and her. Not yet had he spoken to her, but he meant to do so before the show moved on.

Then Rowland cursed hotly as with blaring high-powered horn the car behind suddenly drew level with him, headlights blazing wildly. Instantly he swung his own steering wheel madly to the right, bounced crazily on uneven banking.

With bitter eyes he stared at the sedan momentarily level with him, clearly illumined in the reflecting headlights. He caught a glimpse of a dark, swarthy face under a soft hat. The face was leaning low over the steering wheel, oblivious to everything save demoniacal speed. But that was not all! Rowland nearly over-turned his car in amazement at the transient vision that followed.

For one clear instant he caught a view of a girl beside the driver, head of golden hair dropped heavily back on the leather cushions with all the indications of unconsciousness. Across her mouth was a tight band, obviously a gag. Then the car was on its way, thundering and bumping on in clouds of dust into the dark.

'Helen! Helen Vane!' Rowland breathed mechanically. 'In that car! I'd know her face anywhere!'

He twisted his car to the road level and for nearly two miles kept the sedan in sight. Then it suddenly veered off the lonely country road and went zigzagging away along a barely defined path across open fields. Its rear light presently vanished, perhaps because the driver realized he was being followed. Rowland promptly extinguished his own lights and watched with narrowed eyes through the windshield. The moonlight helped him considerably, enabled him finally to see the car slide into the shade of a massive dark residence, completely isolated from other evidences of habitation.

At that he slowed down, stopped finally within a quarter of a mile of the place and climbed out on the rough road to take stock of the situation.

The solitary residence was surrounded by tall, heavily foliaged trees and high railings. Going closer, Rowland found the massive double front gates locked; beyond them twisted an overhung drive leading into somber darkness.

Not a light gleamed in that lonely place, not a sound came from it; yet within it was surely Helen Vane.

Rowland's lips tightened. He walked the length of the spiked railings and stared between them in some surprise at numberless glass structures resembling conservatories, or hothouses, joining the residence. At first sight it might have belonged to a nurseryman, a raiser of trees for estates; except that nurserymen do not kidnap girls and drive like maniacs.

Jeff Rowland didn't hesitate any longer. Exercising care over the vicious spikes, he climbed the railings and dropped into the tree-laden grounds, picked his way between the well-tended flowerbeds. Finally he came to the largest conservatory and stood studying the open-top ventilator. If he could get through that —

The thought was no sooner in his mind than he had gripped an outlet pipe and was shinning swiftly up it. Gaining the glass roof, he knelt carefully on the wooden framework and eased himself forward to the inviting skylight.

To clamber through it and drop into the warmth of the conservatory was only a moment's work.

For a long time he stood tensed and listening, surrounded by a heavy mid-tropical heat; then it gradually dawned upon him that he could hear a soft moaning, a sighing which proceeded from the stifling, vaguely moonlit greenery.

For an unaccountable reason his scalp began to tighten.

The moonlight was casting its pale glow upon sickly green and twining branches, branches of a plant resembling hypertrophied honeysuckle and occupying one large bed to itself. And it was from this that the noises were emanating. Perplexed, Rowland went closer to it, found himself stiffening in frozen amazement as the groaning suddenly changed into the voice of a woman, filled with exquisite anguish.

'Free me! In the name of mercy — free me!'

Rowland stared with popping eyes into the heart of that slimy, sweating hothouse and saw something unbelievably weird — the head and shoulders of a strange woman which projected above the hot, oozing soil; a woman who was, as green as the plant that coiled about her, whose thick hair hung in rippling black folds to the soil. She was buried up to her bosom;

her arms moved weakly with supplicating, serpentine motions. From her lips, contorted by some unbearable agony, spewed desperate entreaties for release.

'Who — who are you?' Jeff Rowland blurted out, bending toward her.

'Release!' she groaned back. 'Release me, I implore you!'

For a moment the idea of quicksand occurred to him — that she was sinking into this green filth. But that didn't explain her nudity or how she had gotten into the midst of this twining mass of plant. He stepped forward determinedly onto the soil. Instantly the quicksand conception was shattered. It was quite normal.

'Quickly!' the woman screamed, writhing in agony. '*Quickly!*'

Rowland nodded promptly, wondering what particular pain was affecting her so violently. Stooping down behind her, he clamped his powerful hands under her armpits and pulled upward with all his power. Something of extraordinary strength seemed to pull him back — something that caused the woman to scream again and again. Once more he pulled and she abruptly came free, sending him stumbling backward to fall amidst the plant's coil. Like a sigh on a breeze the girl muttered two last words.

'Thank God — ' Then her face froze into its expression of unutterable anguish, her eyes glazed and became fixed.

Jeff Rowland, sprawled, immovable, frozen with sick horror at the sight now in front of him. God — the girl had no body below her upper torso! It was completely severed just above the abdomen, leaving green, smothered entrails and complex nerve endings trailing back into the slimy green pit from which he had dragged her.

Now he understood her agony; her mad desire for release. In some inhuman fashion her very body had been provided with roots, linked to the tree itself. She had been a quasi-plant! A deep and deadly sickness stole over Rowland at the thought, and with it the remembrance of Helen Vane. Monstrous! If such a thing were to happen to her — That thought jerked him to his feet, quivering with smoldering rage. Then he looked up sharply as the conservatory was suddenly swamped in brilliance.

'Don't move!' a voice ordered coldly. 'Stand exactly where you are — and raise your hands!'

Slowly he obeyed, waited while footsteps came from behind him around the plant bed. Then he found himself staring into the darkly swarthy face of the man he had seen in the car, the cold black eyes fixed menacingly upon him,

The man smiled bitterly. 'I was wise in expecting you, my young friend,' he remarked dryly. 'I suspected you might follow me in your car. My judgment of human nature was correct, even to your using the conservatory window I opened especially for your benefit. I have been detained in my surgery, otherwise I would have come much sooner to see if you had arrived. I might even have stopped you from ruining my work — .' His black eyes traveled to the dead hulk of the woman, then around the sinuous masses of the weird plant.

'You have meddled quite a deal, haven't you?' he asked slowly. 'Now I shall have to alter my plans — '

'That girl there!' Rowland broke in passionately. 'Who is she? How in hell's name did she get like that? It's — it's vivisection!'

'No — just art,' the man corrected him smoothly. 'I am responsible, of course. My name is Doctor Calvin Kaylor; I am a retired botanical and anatomical surgeon experimenting with new types — types which none of my blasted contemporaries would believe in. The fusion of a human being with a plant! A fusion that you have spoiled, damn you! You tore out the living heart by the roots!'

His cruel eyes settled on the green cavity from which the stump of a girl had been torn.

'Living heart!' Rowland breathed in fascinated horror. 'You don't mean — '

'I mean that that girl was the heart of this plant. She would have grown into a plant woman — a flower of divine beauty. It means I shall have to start all over again.'

'Not with Helen Vane!' Jeff Rowland shouted frantically. 'Oh, I know you've got her here — that's why I came! You can't do such things, damn your black soul!'

Dr. Kaylor sneered coldly. 'There's plenty I can do, so get that straight. I have Helen Vane here, yes. My intention was to use her for quite a different experiment, but thanks to your infernal meddling she will have to take this girl's place. The plant will die, otherwise. Later I may find a similar use for you — probably you can take the place of Helen Vane in my other experiment . . . Now turn around and get going, through that door! Go on!'

Rowland's fingers twitched with the desire for action, but he was no fool. Upon him rested the life of the girl he had admired from afar. He kept his hands up and walked through a long dark passage with the doctor behind him, then under further directions he turned into an apartment that was obviously a surgery, stacked with impeccably clean but nonetheless grim-looking instruments.

Before he could ask any further questions or make any moves, chains and manacles were clamped on his wrists and ankles, holding him tight to the wall. It was not so much himself he was thinking about now as the sight of the limp, nude girl lying on the central operating table, slender body and limbs held firmly in the grip of spotless white.

There was no denying the fact that it *was* Helen Vane, her face still softly made up from her performance in the circus ring!

2

Hothouse Horror

Rowland shuddered.

'So you are wondering what it is all about?' Kaylor asked cynically, coming forward. 'It isn't really so very complicated. I have already told you that I am finding a way to bridge the gap between animal and plant life. I believe that with that plant in the conservatory, a specially matured one, I can foster a new type of living being — a woman born of a plant, who will perhaps one day in the course of evolution give birth to beings like herself. I *know* it can be done!

'That woman you so kindly saved was my first experiment — some village girl whom nobody traced, of course. Her heart was the life of the plant; her bloodstream was the sap; her organisms kept it going. You will remember she was already green herself — '

'You Godless devil!' Jeff Rowland whispered. 'You're nothing but a fiend!'

'How like the words of my contemporaries before I retired here to work in secret,' Kaylor sneered. 'I think — '

He broke off and moved to the operating table as Helen groaned faintly and squirmed in her bonds.

'So you've recovered?' Kaylor asked bluntly.

At that she jerked her head up, twisted her face around and stared at Jeff Rowland, apparently without recognition. He felt a trifle put out; he was convinced he had attracted her attention from the front row of the circus. Evidently the state of her mind had banished all thoughts and memories.

'What's — what happened?' the girl asked weakly, her eyes dilating in sudden horror as she beheld her unclothed form and buckled straps.

'I'm Dr. Kaylor,' returned the scientist coldly. 'I first saw your photograph in a paper advertising your circus when it visited Philadelphia. I kept track of you until the show came near here. I saw your show three nights ago and decided then that you were just the type I wanted for my work — blonde, healthy and young.

'Tonight I captured you outside your van just after your act — gave you chloroform and brought you here. Unfortunately, the original purpose of my kidnapping you goes for nothing; I have other uses for you now. You can blame this man here,' and he nodded his head toward Rowland.

The girl's face fixed in an expression of deadly fear. She squirmed and twisted helplessly in the straps. Rowland tore on his chains with the ferocity of a maddened animal, aching to get his fingers on this fiend, this monster with the ridiculous excuse of a plant woman. But was it an excuse? The memory of the severed woman returned to his mind in a sudden wave of nausea.

'Kaylor, for God's sake let her go!' he screamed hoarsely. 'I beg of you to do that!'

The surgeon-botanist was not even listening. His eyes were fixed on the helplessly writhing girl.

'I want your body, your heart — your life,' he breathed. 'And I shall have them! Nobody can get into this house without my knowing it. Nobody except this man knows you are even here. I chose my time well — Yes, you will be a very beautiful experiment, my dear!'

Kaylor stood gloating over her, watching the straining of her soft limbs, the wild terror in her staring blue eyes. Then suddenly jerking into life, he wheeled an anaesthetic machine into view, swiftly moved the switches, and clamped the cone over the girl's face.

Jeff Rowland watched with surging passion as Helen Vane twisted and wriggled frantically, gulped and shouted hoarsely under the cone. The straps left crimson welts on her skin as she tugged against them. Then her struggles grew weaker; for the second time that night she relaxed into complete unconsciousness. After a while Kaylor removed the cone and stood regarding her once more.

'It makes it difficult, being the only man who knows the secret of my work,' the surgeon remarked, grinning ghoulishly as he washed his hands in antiseptic fluid. 'I cannot have assistants. However, I think she will remain senseless for the next ninety minutes, and I'll be through by that time.'

'Through?' Jeff Rowland choked. 'In heaven's name, Kaylor, what are you going to do? If you touch that girl — ' he threatened.

'Don't be a damned fool,' the surgeon cut in harshly. 'There is no sentiment in my business. You'll watch this through, and see for yourself what will shortly happen to *you*!'

Rowland fell into a stunned, dead silence, heart thudding against his ribs. His horror began to mount as floodlights suddenly came up over the table and bathed the girl in their shadowless brilliance. Kaylor slipped quickly into sterilized overalls, again washed his hands and then donned rubber gloves. Finally, when fully masked, he moved a spotless instrument tray forward and began to tabulate his various glittering devices, made sure they would be at hand as fast as he needed them. His single-handed operation promised to be a feat of no mean skill.

Jeff Rowland felt that he would go mad with fury and terror as he watched, as he struggled and battled and realized his own helplessness. Finally he was forced to give up from sheer exhaustion, stood sweating and cursing and staring in his shackles as Kaylor got swiftly to work with his keen-bladed scalpel. The vicious blade sliced cleanly into the body in front of him, sliced through the outer skin and drove deep inwards, severing arteries and veins that were promptly sutured. By degrees the ghastly truth ate into Rowland's spinning brain. Kaylor was keeping his word! He was making Helen Vane like that other unhappy girl; was cutting her body into two sections just above the abdomen, making swift and complex nerve connections, changing the entire circulatory movement, performing feats of manipulation that clearly showed he was indeed a surgeon of surpassing skill.

Kaylor finished at last and reverently surveyed the upper half of the body he had divided. The lower half he removed and carried to a place unknown. Then he returned quickly, unfastened the upper half and carried it from the surgery, leaving behind him a trail of newly spilt blood that made Rowland shrink in nauseated horror.

It seemed hours before Kaylor returned, and when he did he was grinning in cruel satisfaction, stripping off his rubber gloves. Then he tugged out his revolver and held it in a rock-steady grip.

With his free hand he snapped Rowland's manacles loose and held him at arm's length as the prisoner tensed to attack him.

'Better not!' Kaylor advised in a level voice. 'It won't get you any place. Get moving into the conservatory — and don't try any tricks!'

Hot with fury Jeff Rowland obeyed and finally entered that warm expanse of light. His eyes turned instantly to the body of the unhappy girl, sunken to her breast as her now vanished predecessor had been in the self-same green pit. She was still alive; the slow but weakened movements of her chest showed that, but her head hung with the heaviness of total unconsciousness.

Kaylor approached the girl. 'Anaesthetic not yet passed off,' he murmured, brooding over her thoughtfully. 'I have connected her arteries and nerves to the corresponding ones in the plant. This plant has a circulation of its own and needs her heart to keep it going. Once her body becomes adjusted, she will rapidly change and start to grow, blossom into something rare and beautiful — a plant woman!

'In heaven's name let's get out of here,' Rowland groaned, turning his face away. 'It's more than I can stand.'

Kaylor chuckled. 'Weakling!' he sneered.

They returned to the corridor, and the next thing Rowland realized clearly was of being flung into an empty, dusty room, and being shackled by long lengths of chain to an immense stake driven deep in the floor.

'Don't worry — I'll look after you,' Kaylor remarked cynically, his face painted into hideous shadows by the electric torch he held in his hand.

'You don't think you can get away with

this, do you?' his prisoner demanded, glaring up at him. 'They'll come looking for that girl, and for me, Kaylor. My car's not far away. If anybody finds it — '

'Thanks for telling me,' the scientist remarked. 'I'll move it into my garage. This house is safe enough, don't you worry. Anybody nosing in here will get plenty for his trouble — Well, I'll see you later — tomorrow morning, in fact,' he sneered.

With that he was gone, leaving Rowland utterly alone. Not very long afterward he heard the noise of his car being driven up the drive, then a silence fell on the terrible house . . .

Rowland awoke from a stiff and drafty slumber on the following morning to discover Kaylor, standing beside him in the drab light filtering through the barred window. Amazingly enough the surgeon was holding quite a respectable-looking breakfast tray in his hands.

'Better eat it,' he advised curtly, setting it down on the floor. 'I'm not doing it for love, but because I want my next subject to be as healthy and well fed as Helen Vane.'

Rowland winced at thought of the outraged girl, but he ate ravenously. He had to keep his strength up in preparation for attacking this fiend when the chance came. When he had finally finished he was released from the shackles, but held once more under the revolver threat, forced to visit that abominable hothouse again. To his surprise green blinds were drawn over the glass windows, plunging the place into deep emerald twilight.

'Light hurts her,' Kaylor muttered almost sympathetically. 'She has changed amazingly in the night, performed a rapid metabolism. When I came in this morning she had her arms over her face to shut out the glare. Once I drew the shades she lowered them, and I could study her carefully. She's turned out a perfect specimen. Look for yourself!'

Rowland didn't need any command, aided as it was by a prod from the revolver. His eyes were already fastened on the incredible sight of that girl, oddly changed in appearance now by reason of her skin having become shiny green, her golden hair deep jet black. Her soft arms were waving gently to and fro in a fashion that was somehow sinuously repulsive — a reptilian tendency following closely the sinuous formation of the ghastly plant of which she was now a part.

Nor did the girl appear to be suffering any.

'It's ghastly,' Rowland groaned, thinking of the Helen Vane he had known and comparing her to this incredible creature writhing in the soil.

'Horrible, nothing! You're just squeamish,' Kaylor growled. 'I guess you've seen enough for now. Back to your room!'

Bitter-faced, Rowland obeyed.

In the room once more the chains and manacles went back on his wrists and ankles.

'I'll be back later,' Kaylor said coldly as he went out and locked the door with a bang.

For a time Rowland sat on the dirty floor trying futilely to conceive some method of escape.

Finally he shook his head wearily and stared helplessly toward the bars of the window.

3

The Woman Grows!

During the day Kaylor came into the room twice to bring food. His final visit was at nine o'clock at night, bringing supper and a camp bed.

'The better you are in health, the better I'll like it,' was his cold comment, as he fixed the cot in position. 'I'll see you tomorrow morning. Sleep well, and don't try anything funny.'

With that the door closed and locked behind him. Rowland ate in silence, surprised to find how hungry he was. Once he had finished he threw himself on the bed, cast the chains as far from him as possible and gave himself up to thought. Finally he slept . . .

About midnight he awoke abruptly at a sudden peculiar sound. The noise was like soft, panther like footfalls — certainly not the brisk steps of Dr. Kaylor. Rowland heard the sound glide past the door of his prison, soft and indefinable.

'Hey, who's there?' he shouted, sitting up. 'Who's there? Let me out of here, whoever you are!'

There was no response to his request. The soft footsteps gradually receded into silence. But only for a while; then minutes later they came again, and again they receded. Quiet returned and saturated the house. Jeff Rowland found himself sweating in sudden fear, fear of the thought that perhaps the plant woman was responsible for the sounds. But that simply could not be! Why, she was rooted breast deep in soil, her entrails joined to the plant itself.

He clenched moist palms tightly, then again he sat up with a jerk as the cloying odour of a peculiar perfume began to waft into his nostrils. In some way it was like acacia and hyacinth mixed together, heavy and exotic, almost indecent in its seductive aroma. Could it be possible that *she* was giving off this heavy mesmeric odour?

Four doors away in his library adjoining the surgery, Kaylor too became aware of the perfume and looked up sharply from the botanical treatise he was studying. Like Rowland, his mind went instantly to the woman he had turned into a plant. And with that thought the first naked crawling of fear became deeply rooted in the depths of his mind.

He knew already that he had outraged all the laws of nature in trying to bridge the gap between human and plant life. Suppose that this new life happened to be charged with immeasurable differences, possessed of inflexible cruelty beyond human understanding? He shuddered. Finally he went to the door and opened it, to find that the corridor reeked with the weirdly seductive odour.

For an instant Kaylor paused; then picking up his revolver he walked swiftly along to the conservatory and entered, switching on the single green-shaded bulb. His heart missed a beat as he saw his strange creation had visibly grown nearly a foot higher out of the soil!

Kaylor stared at her, then suddenly there came from between her greenly lighted teeth a low wailing — the most ghastly blood-freezing wail he had ever heard! It strained his nerves to the breaking point as it sighed and sobbed through the conservatory like an unearthly moaning from the very depths of hell.

In response to the eerie wail something stirred the tree. Its branches visibly moved with horrible, mysterious life. Again the cry issued from the plant woman's parted lips, and again the tree responded with a life that was terrifyingly all its own.

'What have you done?' Kaylor demanded hoarsely, at last of the living statue. 'Speak, if you can! What have you done to my plant? It didn't live and move like this before *you* became a part of it! Oh God, this perfume!' He clenched his fists and tried to choke down the power of that seductive perfume.

The woman's teeth showed again in an unholy smile.

'You made me into a plant and destroyed in me all that was human,' she whispered softly. 'I am glad now. I know things that are not known to mortals. You have given life to formerly immovable plants, Doctor Kaylor. For that I love you — love you deeply!'

Perspiration dewed the surgeon's brow with the intensity of his self-mastery.

'You — you can't talk of things like love,' he muttered hoarsely. 'You're just a plant — '

He broke off and stared as her mouth formed again into a round 'O' and emitted once more that horrible wail. With that his nerve deserted him. He hurtled from that dankly perfumed glass house, with the vision of sinuous, coiling tree branches rooted in his aching brain.

Kaylor gained his library in double-quick time and slammed the door, stood trying to calm his pounding heart. In his own room Jeff Rowland heard Kaylor's hasty retreat, and fell to wondering, not knowing what had happened.

Then he set to work again on his chains, until fatigue and cramping pain got the better of him. In the chill and heavily odorous early hours he fell asleep, and dreamed of the horror that was slowly biting into his every nerve fiber.

The following day was drear and

forlorn. Gray clouds scudded over the heavens; sweeping blankets of misty rain poured across the fields and seemed to gather in solitary menace about the lone house.

Dr. Kaylor was obviously shaken by the events of the night. Rowland could see it in his black eyes. When he brought the food in during the day, his hands were trembling.

'Jitters?' Rowland asked, as he watched them.

'No,' came the angry retort. Then the surgeon straightened up and fell to thinking. 'Did you smell anything in the night?' he asked finally.

'Only perfume,' Jeff Rowland replied, munching steadily. 'It seems to have gone now.'

Kaylor drew the back of his hand over his brow. 'Yes, it's gone now,' he agreed tonelessly. 'But tonight it may come back — '

He said no more then, but went out with his head bowed in thought. He looked only once into the conservatory from the safety of the door and beheld his plant woman even taller, now nearly five feet high from the ground, sinuous arms still twining, mouth ready to form into that ghastly moaning wail — Kaylor beat a hasty retreat.

Ever and again throughout that drear day the surgeon heard that ghastly cry from the conservatory. It penetrated the walls and filled the air with its strange meaning. Once Rowland heard its muffled echo, and the sound struck an odd chord in his memory. Weird and ghastly though it was, he was convinced it was not altogether an alien sound to him. But he had no time to dwell on it; his desperate efforts with the manacles seemed to be getting somewhere at last.

By the time five o'clock had arrived he had worked his right hand free; withdrawn it, raw and bleeding, from the steely clutch that had held it.

Nevertheless, he kept the hand out of sight as Kaylor entered with his supper. It was no use starting anything until he had the left one free, too, and that would take some hours yet. After that, he had only to snap back the ankle fetters and go to work on the surgeon when the opportunity offered. He was thankful when Kaylor left him again to his own devices.

As darkness began to fall, Kaylor's courage waned in proportion. The horrible wailing from the greenery was increasing; probably 'she' needed food. Then as the twilight gave slow place to black night, the perfume returned to roll in reeking waves from the conservatory itself.

Kaylor spent most of the evening in the security of his study, with all the lights blazing behind drawn curtains. He could feel his courage slipping — so much so that he finally jumped to his feet and grabbed his ever-handy revolver. Either he had to shoot that damned woman and ruin the experiment, or else lose his very reason! This haunting dread of something ghastly about to happen, 'her' very presence in the conservatory, were things he could no longer bear.

With tight lips he flung open the door and strode into the perfumed corridor, went swiftly along its drafty darkness and entered the hothouse, switching on the green-shaded light. His nerve began to fail him again, his revolver hand drooped.

The woman was still there, of course, relaxed now for a change. Her hypnotic eyes fixed upon the surgeon from the shadows. Her lissome arms hung down at her sides, fingers nearly touching the soil. Then after a while she began that swaying motion once more, sinuous and seductive. The perfume radiated from her once again in sickening, overpowering waves. And presently that low wailing sob rolled from her heavy scarlet lips.

'In heaven's name, stop that screaming!' Kaylor cried, as the twisted green branches of the devil plant writhed in rhythmic response. 'Stop it, I tell you!' He stood breathing hard, revolver levelled. 'I came here to kill you.' he went on thickly. 'Yes, destroy you — ' He broke off as peal after peal of hideous laughter spewed from her sensuous mouth.

'Kill *me*!' she cried at last in derision. 'First you destroy all within me that is human — change me into a hybrid, half woman and half plant, then you decide to kill me. You ignorant, stupid fool! Don't you realize that it is too late to do that? Hundreds of seeds of me are now in this plant — will blossom in the future, giving hundreds of reproductions of *me*! If you kill me it will make not the slightest difference — there will be perpetual reminders of me, haunting you to the end of your days!'

Kaylor's face blanched. 'You're lying!' he shouted abruptly, voice harsh with fear. 'You've *got* to be lying! What you say is unthinkable! Damn you, for your beauty, your perfume, your unworldly seductiveness! If you don't die I shall lose my reason — '

He stopped suddenly and whirled about at the sound of a thunderous crash in the corridor outside. Even as he stood bewildered, it was followed by another. Quickly he made for the prison door, but at that identical second Rowland catapulted through it, face frozen with fury, bleeding fists clenched for action.

Without a pause his right fist came up and smashed Kaylor under the chin, sent him flying backward. Kaylor's revolver exploded into the air but his grip on it remained unshaken.

'Now you'll get what's coming to you!' Rowland panted, lunging forward. 'Get up, damn you! I'm going to beat you to a pulp, you — '

He broke off short as Kaylor suddenly vaulted to his feet, gun ready for action. He fired — and missed, followed it up with a swinging left haymaker. Rowland sidestepped and brought up a terrific uppercut, hurtling forward to follow up his advantage. But Kaylor's bunched knuckles struck him with blinding force between the eyes. He went reeling backward, felt the sharp stab of a bullet as it tore like white-hot wire across his shoulder. Weakly he dropped down near the now relaxed and brooding plant woman.

He could not be sure, but it seemed to him that she aided him to rise. He felt his injured shoulder and stood swaying, staring groggily at Kaylor's levelled gun. The surgeon was smiling viciously.

'Fine spirit,' he said softly. 'I don't want to kill you — you will be too useful alive. Come over here — '

4

Horrible Revenge

Wincing with pain, eyes narrowed for the slightest sign of a loophole, Jeff Rowland obeyed the command, and this time Kaylor was relentlessly on his guard. He backed around menacingly as Rowland moved, so intent on his task that he failed to notice how close he was coming to the weirdly waving plant woman. The perfume from her body increased by the moment as he stepped further backward in a half circle.

'Sit down there and don't try any tricks!' Kaylor snapped out at last, pointing the gun toward an upturned flower tub. 'I'll deal with you later!'

He paused, half in surprise, as he suddenly became aware of a slim but amazingly firm green hand gripping his revolver wrist.

'You!' Kaylor gasped almost foolishly,

staring up into the lustrous eyes of his creation and feeling the warmth and perfume that seemed to ooze from her. 'I — Let go!' He snapped out the last words savagely, suddenly realizing what was taking place.

Rowland leaped up from the tub, intent on finishing the work he had started, but to his vast surprise — and Kaylor's — the voice of the woman warned him back!

'Stand exactly where you are! Kaylor belongs to me! Obey, or it will be the worse for you!'

Sudden fear wrenched at Kaylor's heart. The plant woman's left hand had come now to join the right. It closed fondly about his throat. The heavy scarlet lips came toward his; fragrant breath blew on his heated face.

Then his horrified gaze became fixed as in response to her suddenly resumed wails the tree became abruptly alive. Some of its sinuous branches began to twirl horribly, writhing and twitching in a revolting fashion like a giant octopus. From the midst of the tangle there presently rose one vicious head, swaying with indescribable menace. Jeff Rowland gulped and stared — why, the thing was a viper! A Viper in *this* plant? It moved sinuously downward to coil about the woman's smooth shoulders, rearing its wicked little head in the perfumed air.

Kaylor's agonized eyes stared at it unbelievingly, then he renewed his frantic efforts to escape. God — a serpent, spawned of this plant, was not even attempting to hurt the woman! True, Helen Vane had once trained and befriended snakes. Was it possible that she was now actually spawning them as plant branches? Incredible!

Calvin Kaylor, traitor to medicine, felt he was going mad. And as he struggled frantically in the woman's immovable grip, he saw heads of other snakes wriggling and twisting in the green gloom, realized that most of the plant branches *were* snakes of all descriptions — puff-adders, cobras, even the deadly fer-de-lance!

Then indeed his heart went sick with horror as he caught a glimpse of a massive main stem twitching and sliding toward him with an immutable inevitability. He screamed wildly, tore and struggled with insane ferocity, but there was something about those slender hands on his wrist and neck pulse that held him in a vise of agony. The slightest movement sent sheer torture pounding through him. With bulging eyes, her face staring down into his, he listened to the screaming wail from those lips, and saw reptilian death squirming toward him!

Jeff Rowland jerked his eyes away from the snakes coiling about the woman to the thing Kaylor was staring at — and his heart missed a beat. What had been the trunk of the plant woman was actually a reawakened boa constrictor! Aroused now by the woman's cries, it slid along with easy swiftness, a full eight feet in length, and presently coiled itself gently but irresistibly about Kaylor's threshing feet, binding them immovably together.

Only then did the woman release the surgeon and stand there, watching implacably. Kaylor screamed in mad pain and horror as that slimy length slid in cold filthy tautness about him. Tighter drew the coils, and far tighter, encircling his waist, his chest, his neck. Breath ceased to enter his lungs. His face turned purple with the constriction

'Remember Helen Vane,' muttered the plant woman, implacable in her hatred.

Rowland turned away, sickened, and listened in silent horror to the racking rend of bones under the snake's frightful power. Kaylor died horribly, mangled by a pitiless foe.

Only when he was a crushed, dying pulp on the floor did the plant woman wail again, this time with a different note. In response the constrictor slid reluctantly from its victim and crawled back to its former position One by one the remaining serpents uncoiled and slid back to the branches.

Rowland twisted around and watched blankly, unbelievingly, as he saw the woman make a sudden effort and rise from the pit! She stood revealed for a moment as a perfect figure in an amazingly tight but elastic substance that covered her to the ankles. Beneath them were incongruous rubber shoes!

With a faint but bitter smile she hobbled from the plant bed and reached up to the electric light bulb, sliding off the green shade. In the return of white light Rowland stared at her incredulously. She was smothered in green grease paint; her black hair was drawn over her breast in sudden modesty. Her eyes were mascaraed into big circles, her lips were laden with lipstick — even perfume still radiated from her. But of one fact there was no possible shadow of doubt — *she was Helen Vane*!

She smiled at him rather wearily as he stood gaping, unable to credit his senses.

'I don't know your name, but your face is familiar,' she said quietly. 'You are the one who watched my act at the circus every night from the front row, aren't you?'

'Why, yes, but — I'm Jeff Rowland,' he stammered. 'But look here! I saw you cut in half by this butcher here — '

'Not me — my sister Marjorie,' she interrupted in a low voice. 'She was my twin, and resembled me. But there were certain differences at close range. That was why I pretended I didn't like white light and had this place made subdued. White light would have given things away.'

She broke off and turned aside, calling loudly. In response the main skylight of the roof rose up and a group of men's faces appeared.

'All over,' she said curtly. 'Take him away. I'm through with this fiend. He's dead.'

The men nodded, and Rowland wonderingly watched as they tossed down a rope ladder and entered the conservatory, bringing with them various boxes and commencing to coax the snakes into them.

'My snakes, of course,' the girl murmured, turning back again. 'You know that I train them because of my circus act. The fangs are drawn on all of them. You see, in my display of magic, which comes before my snake act, my sister helps me — or rather she did. She resembled me closely, especially with make-up, so of course it made many disappearing acts very baffling. This devil here captured her in the circus grounds from outside our caravan. Why, I don't know.'

'He mistook her for you,' Rowland answered grimly. Kaylor was a biological and botanical fiend with a mad obsession — maybe brought on by the constant derision of his contemporaries.'

The girl's eyes were thoughtful. 'Evidently he mistook Marjorie for me because he'd only seen me from the distance of the circus ring,' she said. 'Anyhow, some of the boys saw him carrying her off in his car. They called me right away and we followed the tracks to this place. That wasn't very difficult, with the cross-diamond tire tread he used. For some reason the conservatory roof was open — '

'For me,' Rowland nodded, and briefly explained. 'He must have forgotten to close it again in his excitement.'

'Well, anyhow, I climbed up on the roof and was just in time to see this fiend planting my poor sister in the soil, I heard his words to her, of course — all that he expected she was going to do. When things finally calmed down — after you'd been in to see her, too — I climbed inside and found she was stone dead, horribly, brutally murdered.'

The girl paused and shuddered at the recollection. Then she went on again slowly.

'The very fiendishness of her death did something to me. I went outside again and told the boys; they were all for rushing this place and tearing Kaylor limb from limb, but I wanted to make him suffer as my poor sister had done. I would give up everything to do that. So I developed my idea.

'We returned to the circus and collected my snakes, together with other odds and ends — a rope ladder, make-up box, and so forth. In the night all was quiet. We got into this conservatory again and removed poor Marjorie's remains for decent burial. The snakes we fixed up in this plant. Then I stripped myself to the waist and put on this elastic sheathing, used in my professional work. Green grease paint did the rest. My own make-up was easy, especially with this

166

black wig. The boys took the tackle outside and one or other of them was always around on guard, in case things got too hot.'

Helen Vane smiled bitterly. 'Since Kaylor wanted a plant woman, he should have one. I stood in this pit with galoshes on my feet and mackintosh wrapped around my legs — standing a little higher every time, to convey the idea of growth. In the intervening times I simply sat down and waited for my chance to come. I nearly managed it the first time. You see, I wanted him to come close enough to enable me to get a ju-jitsu grip on him. But at first he was too wary. Once I had him in my grip, the boa would finish the job; I knew that. When he threatened to shoot me tonight, I was in a tight corner, but fortunately you blundered in and saved everything.'

'But the perfume? The wailings by day? The corridor noises?' Rowland asked, puzzled.

'The perfume was nothing much — only a gag to heighten the illusion. I had two full bottles of cheap essence of acacia in my make-up box. A little goes a long way. Last night I emptied a whole bottleful in the corridor. I heard you call, but I did not release you because my vengeance had still to be gained. Of course, I soaked myself in perfume as well. A sweetish odour of that sort can be very suggestive to a man in Kaylor's state of mind — especially if it comes from a supposed plant woman. As to the wailings, they were merely to keep the snakes awake. They know my particular call, of course.'

Jeff Rowland looked at her thoughtfully. 'Now I know where I heard those sounds — at the circus,' he muttered. 'But they were less horrible there, perhaps because the area was bigger. You took a long chance.'

Her shoulders shrugged. 'I was prepared to risk anything, even my life, to avenge Marjorie. The law could only give that fiend the chair — I wanted something more potent. Nobody will ever know what killed him . . . As to my professional act, it's ruined.'

Rowland remained silent for a moment.

Then he patted her arm.

'Maybe it'll work out all right,' he said gently. 'I wanted to meet you, you know — but not like this. Let's get out of this damned place. My car's somewhere around outside. Maybe we'll think up something together.'

They did think up something. Bereft of her sister and finding her snakes always gave her poignant memories of that hideous night in the conservatory, Helen Vane became Mrs. Jeff Rowland in the course of healing time.

7

BOOMERANG

If this confession should ever get out of my prison cell I hope it may serve as a warning to those who think they can cheat Fate. It just cannot be done — and I am the proof of it.

The trouble started when I boarded the train at Edinburgh one icy January evening. I was feeling bitter, depressed, and generally sick of everything. My husband had deserted me when we had seemed to be so happy together; money had almost come to an end — so there was apparently nothing else for it but for me to return to my native heath of London and try to find employment. Anything for a fresh start.

I had been seated in a corner of the compartment for about ten minutes, drowsy after the walk through the cutting Scottish air, when my rather vain hope of a corner to myself was shattered by the arrival of a young woman of about my own age from the corridor outside. Noisily she flung her traveling case up beside me on the rack, then she settled down in the opposite corner.

I watched her lazily through my eyelashes, too comfortable to essay much movement. She was dark, like myself — and, unlike myself, very well dressed. Of similar build, I daresay we would have passed as sisters anywhere.

Presently the train got on the move and the gradual crescendo of clicking joints in the rails, the gentle swaying of the carriage, and the night outside the windows opposite the corridor lulled me completely. I would have dropped asleep had not a sudden thud awakened me.

My half opened eyes settled on my traveling companion's handbag. It had slipped to the floor with the movement of the train, spewing forth all its contents. Before the girl's hands could retrieve it I noticed a wad of five and ten pound notes — there must have been several hundred pounds worth — a small automatic, a powder compact, a bunch of keys, and a scattering of about half a dozen visiting cards upon which was the name of Dorothy Eaton. The address I could not quite make out . . .

But there was something else! The most amazing thing! A snapshot of my husband, David! David, who had deserted me for no apparent reason!

No apparent reason indeed! Now it was clear. He had deserted me for this over-painted, overdressed female by the name of Dorothy Eaton! For *this* I had been flung to the wall!

The clicking of the wheels drummed in my brain. My eyes jerked from the snapshot to an automatic lying amidst the fallen conglomeration . . . An automatic?

Faster clicked the wheels, with ever increasing rhythm. Two bridges sighed past and were gone. We two women were in a world of our own.

Then, much to Dorothy Eaton's surprise — and to a certain extent my own — I was helping her to pick the articles up. I helped her scoop back everything into the handbag — except the automatic. This I retained in my hand. Slowly she put the handbag on the seat beside her and gazed at me fixedly.

The wheels blurred into a crescendo of rattle as we swung over points. Lurching from side to side we two women fixed each other. The roof light glinted on the gun.

'I'd like my automatic, please.' Dorothy Eaton's voice was just a little nervous.

For answer I pulled the blinds down against the corridor side. A plan had formed in my brain in those few seconds of appraisal — a cold, ruthless plan.

'This your gun?' I asked in a low voice, and my heart was thudding along with the wheels.

'Yes, of course. I have a license for it. I'm alone a good deal, and — '

'Except when you're with my husband!' I interrupted, and it was a sheer joy to see the colour fade and betray the rouge on her cheeks.

'You're Sheila Lacy!' she said hoarsely, staring at me 'Sheila Lacy! How did you get in here with me?'

'Pure chance — Heaven sent! So, you are the one who got me into this mess! You sit there in your fancy clothes and with a roll of notes, while I don't know which way to turn! But *I've* got the gun . . . See! Here! In my hand!'

'Don't be a fool,' she whispered, her breast heaving up and down as her heart obviously raced. 'I couldn't help Dave liking me, could I? Besides, I've left him now! That's why I am on this train. I'm returning to London. We had an awful row, and — '

Her voice was drowned out for a while as the train rushed onwards over a water trough.

'I'm not interested in you, or Dave!' I snapped. 'All I *am* interested in is in paying you back — with interest! Like this!'

And before I realized it I had pulled the trigger of the automatic. Above the roar of the train as she took up water the report was muffled somewhat. I saw a red patch defile the white of Dorothy Eaton's blouse just above the heart — and it began to spread. She just sat on, staring at me unblinkingly.

My pulses were going like trip hammers now in sympathy with the wheels on the rails. Gradually I began to realize what I had done. Leaning across I gripped her pulse. She was dead. My one shot must have gone right through her heart.

'Tickets! Tickets please!'

Great God, now what? The inspector was only two compartments away. Somehow I kept myself calm, for I had a plan — but it would demand plenty of nerve ... At top speed I searched the dead girl's handbag and found her ticket. Then, heaving her into her corner seat I pulled her costume coat well over her bloodstained blouse and left her in a sleeping position with her head drooping forward. When the inspector looked inside in the dim light I sat on the automatic and handed him two tickets.

As he handed the tickets back he looked at me keenly.

'Everything all right in here, miss?'

I felt myself becoming suddenly hot. 'All — all right?' I repeated, trying to sound casual. 'Why surely. Why not?'

'Oh, nothing; I'm asking them all the same thing in this part of the train. I thought I heard a sort of crack from somewhere about here. Maybe a stone against one of the windows as we took up water.'

'I expect that would be it,' I agreed, and with that he went out and slammed the door on me.

Now for my plan! I picked up Dorothy Eaton's handbag from the seat opposite and searched through it, pulled out one of the visiting cards and studied it. Dorothy Eaton. So far so good. My next move was simple. I exchanged her bag for my own, except that I retained the money. In my old bag were two visiting cards with my own name on them. To them I added a brief suicide note and signed it with my own name — Sheila Lacy. Then, into Dorothy Eaton's stiffening fingers I fitted the automatic, concealing it by drawing her arm up a little inside her coat. To the casual observer she would seem to be asleep. By the time the truth was found out I would be far away.

The police, I reasoned, would assume it to be real suicide, and since I had been — and still was — wearing gloves only

Dorothy's fingerprints would be on the gun. So few people had known me in Edinburgh that they would probably swear Dorothy *was* me if it came to it. Dave himself would know different, of course, but since enquiry would involve him I reasoned he would be careful how much he said.

I was still vaguely uneasy, though. Finally I dislodged the automatic again from Dorothy's tight hold and examined it — broke it open. Surprisingly, two bullets had been fired. Either I had fired two in my excitement, or else — Well, it didn't signify, anyway. Everything was perfect. So I put the gun back again in that tightening clutch.

And the inspector who thought that he had heard a shot? Well, if anything, that would verify the suicide. The police would be told that I had handed up her ticket as though I were a friend of hers. Quite right — but they would have to find me first to make me a witness. Besides, I would say then that she must have shot herself while I had left the compartment to get some air.

I was Dorothy Eaton now. I possessed nearly five hundred pounds as a basis on which to start anew. I had justifiably killed the woman who had started my troubles — killed her in absolute safety. My scheme was foolproof.

When we got to Euston Station I took down her traveling case and escaped on to the busy platform. I had no trouble at the barrier — but I ran into trouble just beyond it. Two men suddenly came out of nowhere and blocked my path!

'Your name, madam?' the taller one enquired respectfully, and showed me his official card.

Scotland Yard! So they had found out already! Well, I was safe enough.

'Dorothy Eaton,' I answered calmly.

'You are sure of that?'

'Why, certainly. I have one of my cards here — '

I rummaged in Dorothy's bag and handed out one of her visiting cards. The Yard man studied it and then nodded.

'Very good . . . Did you ever know a man by the name of David Lacy?'

For the first time I felt a horrible

qualm. What on Earth had Dave got to do with things?

'Why — yes,' I assented slowly. 'I know him . . . '

'You are under arrest, Miss Eaton, for his murder! He was shot and killed by you in a violent quarrel before you left to catch the London train this evening. Three witnesses can prove it. If you will come this way, please . . . '

I could not speak, or even think. Now I knew where the second bullet had gone! If I denied my identity I would be accused of the murder of Dorothy Eaton — and rightly. Yet if I didn't — ?

Boomerang!

8

LAST EXTRA

At five thirty on a drizzling November Saturday afternoon, a police car sped out of Scotland Yard. At the wheel, skimming through the traffic with his usual nonchalance, sat Sergeant Jim Brown.

Beside him, hat tilted forward over pale blue eyes, Chief Inspector Duxbury chewed on a dead match. Known as 'Old Ironsides' to his intimates because he pursued criminals with iron resolution, he picked up used matches and kept them in an empty box.

'Whoever dialed nine-nine-nine will have vanished into the woodwork,' Duxbury said: 'You can bet on it.'

'We'll find him if we have to, sir.'

'Some hope! Tracing a call from a public box is damned near impossible.'

He became silent, watching the traffic and the wet roads as the car hurtled forward. Brown turned into a narrow back street named Garden Terrace. In the light from street lamps and shop windows, the curious had gathered around the doorway of a pawnshop. The blinds were drawn and a constable stood on duty.

As Duxbury and the sergeant arrived, the constable saluted.

'Get these people moving on,' the Chief Inspector said curtly. 'This isn't an exhibition. And show in the doctor and the crime squad when they get here.'

'Right, sir.'

Duxbury walked into the shop and Brown closed the door.

Silent, peering from under the brim of his hat, Old Ironsides summed up the shop. It was identical to any other pawnbroker's in London — a sales counter, a pledge counter with a steel grille, glass cases filled with watches and jewellery. There were shelves of clothing and blankets — and on the counter, a solitary ox-hide suitcase.

'Ten to one that suitcase isn't part of the stock,' Duxbury said.

Still nibbling on a dead match, he moved behind the counter and looked down at the sprawled body of a middle-aged man. Blood seeped from a crushing blow at the back of the head. Beside him lay a heavy copper candlestick with a blood-spattered newspaper wrapped around the top.

'The body our unknown telephone informant saw,' Duxbury said. 'But he used a public call box.'

'Looks like robbery with violence, sir.'

The Chief Inspector looked at the till. The drawer had been opened and only the coins left. On a shelf below, a metal cash-box had been forced. That was empty, and a heavy poker lay beside it

'Take a look around,' Duxbury instructed Brown. 'Keep your fingers off everything until the experts have finished. We might say the chap who telephoned did this — but I don't go for the idea that a murderer rings up the Yard. He gets out quickly, and silently.'

He began a careful examination of the shop and had got half way through when the doorbell rang and the Divisional surgeon and the crime squad came in.

Old Ironsides nodded to them and

continued his search. Photographers' flash-bulbs blazed; fingerprint men dusted. Duxbury contemplated the oxhide suitcase on the counter, chewing on a match.

He motioned to one of the experts. 'Give this a dusting. I want to take a look at it, and I don't want my dabs on it. While you're going over it, I'll be outside.'

He strolled out into the drizzle, hands in the pockets of his raincoat, and stood beside the caped policeman. Men and women passed, glancing curiously at the shop. A car passed with a swish of tires on wet tarmac. At the end of the street, beneath a lamppost, a newspaper seller shouted:

'Extra, extra! All the football results. Extra!'

Old Ironsides threw away his chewed match and stepped out to look at the pawnbroker's window. In gilt letters under three brass balls, a sign read:

DAVID RUBENSTONE
JEWELLERS AND LICENSED
PAWNBROKER

Duxbury gestured at the constable.

'Find out Rubenstone's address. If he has relatives, tell them to go to the East Aldgate mortuary. By that time the body will be there.'

He turned away and strolled down the street to where the newspaperman was still shouting.

'Paper, sir?'

'No, thanks. Just a few words . . . '

Duxbury showed his warrant card in the light of the gaslamp, and the newspaper seller shrugged.

'Ain't much of a surprise, Inspector. I saw the police car come — some bloke do for Ruby?'

Old Ironsides put his card back in his wallet and sized up the newspaperman. He was tall and wiry, with a cap pulled low over a thin face; he wore a sodden overcoat with baggy flannel trousers.

'By Ruby I suppose you mean Rubenstone. So you knew him?'

''Course I knew 'im. I know everybody in this street. 'Ad many a yarn with the old twister. Why?'

Pale unblinking eyes gave nothing away.

'I'll ask the questions. What's your name?'

'Billy. Billy Horsfall.'

Old Ironsides looked thoughtfully along the street. The door of the pawnbroker's shop was plainly visible.

'Where's the nearest public telephone box?'

'Other end of the street. Someone tipped you off, did they?'

'I'm interested in a suitcase. A man taking a suitcase into Rubenstone's. Did you see anyone like that?'

' 'Course I did. I ain't blind, you know.'

'Describe him.'

'A little man in a threadbare overcoat and greasy bowler 'at. I noticed him particular like 'cause he had this expensive-looking suitcase.'

'Interesting. Now I want you to come back to the shop and look at something.'

'What, now? I've got me job to do.'

'Now,' Duxbury said flatly. 'This is a murder case.'

Grumbling, Horsfall collected his unsold newspapers from under a tarpaulin and tucked them under his arm.

'Can't trust nobody these days. Won't

take long, will it?

'No time at all.'

Back at the shop, Duxbury nodded towards the suitcase on the counter. 'Is this the case you saw?'

'That's it, Inspector. No mistake about it.'

Duxbury opened it and studied the inside. It was empty and obviously brand new. He called the constable.

'From the description, and this suitcase, it sounds like the Ferret. Check with C.R.O at the Yard and get his address. Then bring him here.'

The constable saluted and went out in a flurry of raindrops.

'All right, you can go, Horsfall — after you've given the sergeant your address.'

When the newspaperman had left, Old Ironsides went behind the counter and looked down at the body. He stooped and slowly unwrapped the blood-speckled paper from around the top of the candlestick. Putting the newspaper on the counter, he flattened it out.

'Last extra edition of the *Evening News*, sir,' Sergeant Brown commented.

'Today's date, too.'

'The idea being, of course, to prevent fingerprints getting on the weapon.'

'And this poor devil's been dead for an hour — '

'About an hour,' Duxbury corrected. 'You can't tell to a minute.'

'Anyway, sir, it's not unlikely that the bloke who phoned us did the murder.'

Duxbury raised an eyebrow. 'Go on. Let's have your theory.'

'Take this suitcase,' Brown said. 'I suggest he came to steal stuff and put it in the case. He probably intended to pinch jewelry — then changed his mind and took money instead. So he didn't need the case. Maybe he got scared after killing the old man and didn't want to hang around. So he grabbed the cash and ran.'

'Stopping to ring the Yard and say there was a dead body here?' Duxbury asked dryly. 'Well, it has possibilities, but if the man we want is the Ferret, it doesn't fit. He never murdered anybody in his life — he isn't the type.'

He turned to consider the newspaper again, then folded it carefully in a cellophane bag. He indicated the poker and the candlestick.

'Wrap those up, Jim. We'll need them as evidence after the lab's had them.'

Old Ironsides went back to studying the cash register and the tin box.

'Only money taken apparently,' he murmured. 'That suggests there was enough money to make it worth while. Easier to carry than jewellery, too . . . '

He watched two ambulance men carry the body out on a stretcher.

To Brown, he said: 'Be with you in a moment.'

He went outside and strolled down the street towards the newspaper stand. There were more people about now — some of them taking a short cut to the cinema in the High Street.

'Something happened?' Billy Horsfall asked.

'I've been thinking,' Duxbury said. 'You saw the man with the suitcase — did you see anyone else?'

'Depends about what time?'

'Say four-thirty to five.'

'Four thirty to five? That's about the

time the van left my last extras. Yeah, I remember now. 'Course, quite a few people been in and out of Ruby's today — but this one bloke. He bought an *Evening News* about four o'clock — said he wanted the half-time football results. About an hour later he came back and went into Ruby's.'

'What did he look like?'

'Bit of a toff for this part of town. Tall, well dressed, with fair hair. About thirty-five, I'd say.'

'And you didn't see anyone else go in?'

'Not between him and the bloke with the suitcase.'

Duxbury considered the pile of news-papers under the tarpaulin 'Okay — thanks.'

He returned to the pawnbroker's and went to the counter to examine the records. He ran a finger along the last entry in the ledger. It read:

November 2.

Kenneth Clive, 27 Hilton Street, W.C. 7

Cigarette case. Price paid: £20. Time: 4.58 p.m.

'Today's date,' Brown observed. 'He

could be the Johnny we want.'

Duxbury made a note of the address.

'Except that I wonder why he permitted his name to be recorded before he committed murder. You'd think he'd have killed Rubenstone first. Anyway, we'd better see what he has to say . . . you got the address of Horsfall?'

'Yes sir.'

'We'll have someone keep an eye on him. He's proving useful in this business — and we can't afford to lose a witness. Let's get along and hear what Mr. Clive can tell us.'

As they moved towards the door, it opened and a constable pushed a small man inside. He wore a threadbare overcoat and a greasy bowler hat; he had a fox-like face and blue eyes.

Duxbury gave a slow, cold smile. 'Well, here's the Ferret!'

'He's admitted it, sir,' the constable said. 'That he telephoned the Yard, I mean. C.R.O. had his address and I picked him up.'

'Which I greatly resent,' the little man objected, his face taking on an expression of superiority. 'I helped you, didn't I, by tipping you off to this murder?'

'Where did the suitcase come from?' Duxbury demanded.

The Ferret shrugged. 'If I thought you were going to pick me up, I'd never have tipped you off. Only I can't stand murder — that's why I did it. And what do you do? Insult me by asking about a suitcase . . . '

He drew himself erect. 'I stole it, of course. Nothing easier. It was on show downtown — you know I can't keep my fingers off the leather stuff. So when the bloke's back was turned, I walked off with it. You know my technique.'

'After twenty-seven convictions, I ought to,' Old Ironsides answered. 'And you came here to sell it; I suppose?'

'Naturally. 'When I couldn't get service, I looked behind the counter, saw the body — and panicked. Murder upsets me. Besides, I thought I might get the blame. So I got out fast — forgetting the case — and got to thinking. Was he dead? I'd only seen him lying there with his head battered. Help might save his life, that's why I rang up the Yard. And this is what I get!'

'Did you see anything? Hear anyone?' Duxbury asked.

'No, and that's the truth, Inspector.

Old Ironsides gave a slow nod. 'Yes, Ferret, I'm inclined to believe you. What can you tell me about Rubenstone? Was he a fence?'

'Er — yes,' the Ferret admitted.

'I guessed as much, or else you wouldn't have risked dealing with him. Been dealing with him long?'

'For years — on and off. He was a good man.' The Ferret looked mournful. 'Pity someone wiped him out. Always cash on the nail. Did you know he carried a float of two thousand pounds for hot stuff? He told me about it once. 'Course, he knew he was safe telling me — I only take leather. Leather! That's what I can't resist. Just can't help it.'

'A two thousand cash float for hot stuff,' Duxhury murmured. 'Jewels, I suppose . . . that's interesting. Looks like he told a wrong 'un.'

The Chief Inspector reflected for a

moment, then turned to the constable.

'All right, lock him up. That'll make the twenty-eighth conviction for leather theft.'

He watched as, with serio-comic dignity, the little man was ushered out. The door closed behind the constable's swishing cape.

'You believe him?' Sergeant Brown asked doubtfully.

'I do, Jim. I'd trust the Ferret with thy life. He doesn't lie, or kill or touch drugs — doesn't even steal jewels. He has this strange urge to steal leather. The psychiatrists get gray hairs trying to figure him out. Yes, I think he told the truth — and if he didn't, he'll be in custody if we want him.'

'You're convinced he didn't kill Rubenstone?'

'Use your head, man. Why should he? The fence was the goose that lays the golden eggs as far as the Ferret's concerned. Why should he want to cut off his source of income? What interests me is that Rubenstone kept a two thousand pound float, almost certainly in notes

— fives, tens and twenties perhaps. Wouldn't be difficult to hide that. And someone knew he had that float . . . '

There was silence for a moment, then Sergeant Brown cleared his throat.

'We might find out how much this Kenneth Clive knows about it, sir.'

Old Ironsides nodded and looked at the clock on the wall above the door. He checked it against his watch.

'Only a minute or two out,' he murmured, as they left the pawnbroker's shop.

*　*　*

It was nearly seven o'clock when they reached Kenneth Clive's address. It was a classy street — a bit too classy for a man who had sold a cigarette case for twenty pounds. The mystery was partly explained when they learnt that Clive had only one room in the house.

He ushered the Chief Inspector and Sergeant into his bed-sitter with a troubled solemnity. As the newspaper seller had said, Clive was tall with fair hair, and good-looking with a nervous manner.

'I don't know what this is about, gentlemen,' he said, motioning them to chairs, 'and I'm not sure that I like it either.'

'Unfortunately, Mr. Clive, the law is not concerned whether you like it or not,' Duxbury said dryly. 'I want to know if you visited Rubenstone's, a pawnbroker in Garden Terrace, this evening around five o'clock.'

Surprise showed in Clive's face. 'Why . . . yes, I did as a matter of fact. But what on earth has that to do with you?'

'And you sold a silver cigarette case for twenty pounds?'

The young man coloured slightly. 'Suppose I did? It was my own property. Are you suggesting it was stolen?'

'I'm suggesting, Mr. Clive, that you be careful how you answer my questions,' Duxbury said, pale eyes unblinking. 'For your information, Rubenstone was murdered tonight at approximately five o'clock and, naturally, we're checking up. We got your name from the ledger — you were his last customer.'

'Murdered!' Kenneth Clive gave a little gasp and sat down heavily. He stared blankly at the detectives. 'But — but surely you don't think that I — '

'Why did you choose a pawnbroker so far from your room?'

'So I wouldn't be recognized, of course.' From looking angry, Clive had become uncomfortable. He gestured at the barely furnished room. 'As you can see, I'm down on my luck. I lost my job, and I'm in debt. I need that twenty pounds to help buy necessities.'

'Before you entered Rubenstone's, you bought a newspaper.'

'That's not a crime, is it?'

'What did you do with it?'

'I gave it away.'

'Really?'

'Do you doubt my word?' Clive snapped.

'I didn't say that. Bit generous of you, in the circumstances.'

'I suppose it's your job which makes you suspicious of the simplest action,' Clive said bitterly. 'I knew when I saw the half-time scores that the teams I'd bet on couldn't possibly win. The paper was no use to me after that. I gave it to a chap at the end of the street who asked me what had won the two-thirty race.'

'What sort of chap? Did he wear a bowler hat?'

'I don't think so. Some sort of flat cap. He looked down and out.'

'I see. You gave the paper away at the end of the street. Which end? Where the newspaper man has his stand?'

'No. The other end.'

'And you're certain,' Duxbury asked, 'that you hadn't turned the corner into the main road?'

'Quite sure — if it matters.'

'Did you notice anyone else about? Hear anything suspicious?'

'No.'

'When Rubenstone filled in the ledger, did he refer to a watch for the time?'

'No, he looked at the clock on the wall. It was two minutes fast by my watch.'

'All right Mr. Clive, that'll be all for now. I may want to see you again.'

Old Ironsides and Sergeant Brown left

the house and sat in the car.

'So what's your theory, sergeant?'

'He looks good to me. He admits he's broke and needs money. He had a newspaper — that story about him giving it away to a down and out wouldn't deceive a two year old. And he must have been in the shop, otherwise he wouldn't know about the clock on the wall. You can't see that from the doorway, or outside.'

'But he left his name and address when he could easily have torn that page out of the ledger. Drive back to Garden Terrace — I've one or two things to check.'

Brown only nodded, disgruntled by his superior's lack of enthusiasm for his theory.

The return journey took only fifteen minutes. The narrow back street seemed unchanged, if a little more populated. The lights on the shops opposite had gone out. At the end of the street, Billy Horsfall still shouted, 'Last Extra!'

Duxbury climbed stiffly out of the car and said, 'Fetch Horsfall here.'

As Brown went off, Duxbury entered

the pawnbroker's shop and looked around. He waited till Brown returned with the newspaper seller.

Duxbury took a dead match from the box in his pocket and began to chew on it. His pale eyes fixed their gaze on the bundle of newspapers tucked under Horsfall's arm.

'Still afraid of someone pinching your papers?'

'I've a right to be afraid, ain't I? It's my living, remember.'

Duxbury reversed a chair and sat with his arms folded on the back rest. He considered the newspaperman with brooding intensity.

'Ever hear of a generous policeman, Horsfall?' he asked.

'Generous? Don't make me laugh! I never heard of a generous copper in me life.'

'Clive was feeling generous when he gave his paper to a down and out. Maybe it's catching. I'm feeling generous,' Duxbury said calmly. How many papers have you got left?'

Horsfall glanced at the bundle under

his arm. 'About twenty.'

'Twenty at thirty pence each.' Duxbury took a five-pound note from his wallet, and placed it carefully on the wooden counter. Then he took a pound coin from a pocket and spun it in the air. It landed with a sharp sound on the counter. There was silence for a moment

'Sold to the gentleman with the matchstick,' Duxbury said, and threw away the chewed match.

'I don't do business that way,' Horsfall protested.

'It's a cold wet night. I'm buying the rest of your papers. Now get off home.'

Horsfall looked about him, his expression desperate. Duxbury nodded. Sergeant Brown grabbed the bundle of newspapers and placed them on the counter.

'Clive was in this shop a few minutes before five, and Rubenstone was alive then. He left his name and address. The Ferret was here about fifteen minutes after five, and found a dead body. Not much time for a murderer to slip in and out. It had to be someone who knew the street well. Someone on the spot with his eyes open. I fancy you for the job, Horsfall.'

'It's a dirty lie!' Billy Horsfall shouted.

'When you brought Clive into it, you slipped up. He bought a paper with the half-time scores. Another edition arrived after that — the Last Extra. You told me that yourself — and the paper wrapped around the candlestick was the last edition.'

'That doesn't prove anything,' Horsfall said sullenly.

'But this does.'

Chief Inspector Duxbury picked up the bundle of newspapers from the counter and shook them vigorously. Five, ten and twenty pound notes cascaded to the floor.

As Brown snapped the handcuffs on, Old Ironsides selected a dead matchstick and chewed contentedly.

9

THE STAIN THAT GREW

It was nearing twilight when Calver Mason reached the outskirts of the little Middle West village of Craven Town. In ten minutes he was through the village — a gaunt, sombre figure of a man, cadaverous face set into harshly cut lines, cheeks coated with a three days' stubble. Dust stirred round boots that were deeply down at heel.

Three days and nights he had been walking, motivated by only one desire — vengeance. All sparks of sentiment and manliness had been purged from him when he had at last known the terrible truth. His daughter had been murdered by a fiend. There could no longer be any doubt about it. Viciously, cleverly murdered, so that the police could do little about it. But Calver Mason could — and meant to!

At last he beheld that which he sought. Before him stretched a rugged expanse of mountainous terrain; behind it all lay the blood-red gash of the dying sunset. Silhouetted against this reposed the only two habitations for miles — the one, a tiny cliff-edge shack, and the other an isolated factory closed for the night. Only for an instant did Mason take in the lofty chimney of the factory, survey its silent, darkened windows, then his lips shut as his gaze fell to the solitary shack. So he had tracked Melvin Gorne down at last.

Tireless, waxen of face, he strode up to the place and hammered grimly on the door. For a long time there was no response, then there came a shuffling and the door opened. A bleak, cruel face looked out upon him.

'Mason!' Gorne gasped hoarsely, and made to shut the door. But with one shove of a massive shoulder Mason flung it back on its hinges and strode into the dingy interior.

A small oil lamp was burning, casting a fitful yellow glow upon a scene of chaos. Dirt was in every corner; the floor itself was filthy. A tablecloth, fallen into holes, adorned the battered table. And in the midst of it all Gorne crouched now like a frightened beast, deep-set eyes glowing with the light of madness.

Then, little by little, he seemed to recover himself.

'So this is where you got to, Gorne!' Mason breathed, fixing him with a deadly stare. 'This is the hell-hole to which you dragged my daughter! Through weeks and months I've searched for you — then, a chance clue in New Orleans, an interview with the police — and now I've tracked you down. You murdered my daughter — slew her. And as sure as there is a God you're going to go the same way!'

'Think so?' Gorne sneered, and chuckled harshly. 'I killed your daughter, yes — because she tried to kill me. She hated me, poor dear — didn't like my methods. So I brought her here. She died horribly, Mason — horribly. Slowly strangled to death . . . I buried her corpse just at the cliff edge there. I knew the police would never get me here, even though they had their suspicions. As for you, you can't come here and get away again, Mason!'

'I came to kill you, Gorne, and I mean

to do it,' Mason answered tonelessly, and with that drew out a revolver from his pocket.

But he was not quite quick enough. Days and nights of tramping, of consuming hatred, had drained upon his alertness. He was unprepared for Gorne's sudden tremendous forward leap. It was the leap of a madman. In one sweep he had knocked the revolver from Mason's hand, brought up a skinny fist and planted it straight in his enemy's face. Gasping with the suddeness and pain Mason went flying over backwards.

Gorne laughed shortly, whirled round, and snatched up the heavy iron poker from the ancient log fireplace. Savagely, fiendishly, he whirled it through the air and brought it down with smashing force on Mason's head.

Mason groaned, but for a moment consciousness clung to him.

'May hell curse you, Gorne!' he panted thickly. 'One murder — now another! But I'll return! My blood and soul will return to crush you to perdition!'

Gorne did not wait to hear more. Again

and again he smashed the poker down with maniacal power, did not cease until the body of Mason lay limp and inert on the floor, blood flowing steadily from his crushed head. The poker dropped from Gorne's hand with a clatter. For a space he stared wide-eyed at the corpse, stricken for an instant with momentary sanity.

Then again the madness that was within him returned. He laughed raucously, cast a look round the dingy filthiness of the hovel in which he existed, had existed ever since he had brought his young wife here and murdered her in a fit of insane passion.

For a space he considered, then looked through the open door toward the deserted expanse outside, reaching right to the cliff edge. There in the murky silence of the approaching night lay the crude grave of Mason's daughter. Here was another body to be disposed of. He turned swiftly, picked up a heavy shovel from by the wall, and strode out into the darkness.

Throughout the night, in the complete darkness, whilst the mountain winds wailed about his skinny form, until his back was cracking with the effort, he dug a second grave not twenty feet from the first one. Before the dawn came he seized Mason's stiffened corpse, dragged it along the ground, and dropped it into the cavity he had made. He chuckled to himself at each hollow reverberation of falling earth.

Then at last the hole was refilled and he returned to the shack, slammed the door, bolted it, and from sheer exhaustion fell asleep.

Toward the following evening Melvin Gorne awoke again, ate ravenously from his sparse supplies, and listened as he munched to the sound of the rising gale as it boomed round the old shack. A sense of intense uneasiness, for which he could not account, was upon him. It was the first time he had experienced a gale in these quarters. Usually the climate was fairly quiet and reliable.

Memories of the night before, of the brutal killing of Mason floated into his warped mind. He laughed again, hollowly, and the wind muttered in the rotting gables of the old place.

'My blood and soul will return to crush you into perdition!' That was what it seemed to say, reiterated endlessly, monotonously, like the joints in a railway line. Gorne crushed the liquor glass in his fingers until it collapsed into splinters and he sat like a wounded animal staring at the blood streaming from minor glass cuts.

'No!' he shouted suddenly. 'No! You can't return, Mason! Any more than your daughter can! The dead are forever dead!'

He ceased speaking suddenly, wrenched open the door, and strode out into the night. The wind smote him like something solid, hurtling up the gorge with the roar of a thousand demons. At the same time he was aware of something else — a foul and overpowering stench that had within it all the vileness, the filthy moldering odor of the grave. It was the first time he had ever noticed it, but there was no denying the dankness of the atmosphere. The gale crept with the portent of funereal disaster.

Trembling he gained the recently made

grave and looked at it in the dim light. He tried to strike a match but the wind whipped the flame into extinguishment. Then suddenly the moon shot into view from behind the scurrying clouds and flooded the scene with ghastly, pallid radiance.

Gorne stiffened. Now he could distinctly see a round carmine patch on the yellow soil atop the grave. Blood-red; the size of a melon, perhaps. He bent down to touch it, then something held him back.

'Blood!' he muttered. 'Blood! He said his blood and soul would return — No! Not that! Melvin Gorne, you are a fool! There's nothing at all. And yet — '

His breath caught and he stared again. Behind him in the distance the yellow lights of the isolated factory were dancing through the approaching storm. Tonight they were evidently working overtime in the place.

Stupidly Gorne turned and went back to the shack, the memory of the red stain biting ever deeper into his merciless, half-crazy mind. Every whistle of the wind, every creak of the ancient timbers seemed to reiterate the words of the dying Mason. Time and time again he peered furtively through the window, drew aside the brittle, faded curtains, and every time he pictured in his mind's eyes that stain, blood-red and horribly fresh. The thought of it made him wild.

'It can't be blood!' he shouted into the shadows. 'Blood ceases to flow when a body dies! Calver Mason, you're dead — dead as your daughter!'

He gloated over that. 'You just died a little faster, that's all. She died slowly, just as she deserved.'

He broke off with a sudden start. The wind; a solid, mounting wall of fury suddenly buffeted against the shack wall and flung down an ancient picture from its hook. Gorne sat in silence, licking his dry lips, fingers in his unkempt gray hair, staring at the glass splinters and dust-caked print. Somewhere, he remembered, that that meant a death.

He stood up again, indecisive, then trembling in spite of himself tried to sleep again. Sleep, however, would not come to his overburdened mind. He lay there in the darkness, the lamp extinguished, and thought of the endless miles of storm-swept country that surrounded him. He was alone, save for people in the busily working factory. For a fleeting instant he thought of going there, then remembering that that would probably entail an inquiry he refrained from pursuing the idea.

And, little by little as he lay there trembling, the dirty blanket clutched in his gnarled hands, that same horrible odor he had detected outside floated into the grimy fastness of his retreat. Yes, it *was* from the grave! He was sure of it now. It penetrated into every nook and cranny, a stench that reminded him vaguely of rotting chrysanthemums, filled, too, with an unutterable coldness, unless that was the chill produced by the terrific fear that was governing him.

Somewhere abroad in this clammy dark must be the avenging soul of Calver Mason, waiting, waiting, through the timeless minutes to strike — to crush him into the perdition he deserved.

With a half scream Gorne sat up again and stared with dilated eyes into the blackness. He fully expected to behold the spectral presence of Mason himself, but the darkness remained unrelieved.

For a long time Gorne sat there, then he climbed out of the bed and relit the lamp. His knees were shaking, and they continued to do so even though he cursed himself huskily for a weak and imaginative fool.

Time and time again, furiously though he fought against it, the remembrance of that stain came back to him. Blood — upward, from a dead man! The thing was impossible! Nevertheless the recollection was too strong to permit of only conjecture. He wrenched the door open once more and stumbled out into the blackness. A loose stone caught his foot and sent him sprawling with his face within five inches of the grave itself.

Shuddering horror surged through him. The stain was there, but it was infinitely larger! The soil was saturated with it! Roughly it had formed into the shape of a man, a blood-red, sodden reincarnation of a man.

With a scream Gorne jumped upright,

shouted desperately to the howling wind that flapped his worn garments about his emaciated frame.

'You're coming back, Mason!' he shouted desperately. 'You're coming back! Stop, I tell you! *Stop*!'

His excess of emotion and fright suddenly vanished at his outburst. He became cooler. Momentary sane reasoning plainly indicated that this was absurd. Blood from a dead man? That thought stuck in his mind.

With an obstinate shake of his head he returned to the shack for the shovel. Grimly, resolutely, he drove it down into the red, glutinous mass. A deep shudder shook him at the soggy, ghastly sucking noise the soil made as he lifted a shovelful into the air. Immediately the red stain refilled into position. The crimson drops fell slowly from Gorne's shovel as he stood staring.

Then it was blood! Flowing from a source unknown! Or was it unknown? Deep down in that spot lay Mason's corpse. If it was his blood then his soul must be abroad, too.

It was too much for Gorne. He dropped the shovel with a crash and raced back screaming to the shack, slammed and bolted the door, then sat in sweating horror until the dawn crept through the angry clouds.

Throughout that boisterous day Gorne did not attempt to leave his retreat. He was too frightened. He did take furtive peeps through the window and, every time his eyes were met by that distant carmine stain. It had grown again since the night and covered now the entire area of the grave, its irregular edges steadily spreading towards the older grave of the girl herself.

Still there hung on the air that horrible smell, and it remained with the gale, which showed no signs of abating. Night fell again finally and Gorne was in a pitiable state. His naturally lean face was shrunken almost to that of a skeleton. Eyes filled with the light of insanity stared horribly into the dark.

Still the wind seemed to mutter: 'My soul and blood shall return!'

He did not know how long he sat there

in the darkness, but at last he got to his feet, taking a sudden grip on himself. This mystery had to be solved or he would entirely lose his reason. Stubbornly, resolutely, he opened the door and noted how much stronger was the gale.

Pressing against it, head down, he gained the grave again and stared mutely at the expanse of redness. With every breath he took the musty dank odor filled his nostrils.

'You can't come back!' he shouted fiercely. 'I'll dig you out first!'

He turned to pick up the shovel, but at the identical moment a stronger gust of the wind caught his skinny frame and sent him sprawling backwards. His heels caught in the soggy red mass as he overbalanced. Hoarsely, madly, he screamed, but it was too late.

He lost his balance completely and with a terrible cry fell over the edge of the cliff and dropped a sheer thousand feet into the gale-ridden canyon below.

And above, the stain steadily spread . . .

★ ★ ★

Danvers, City Editor of the New Orleans *Observer*, surveyed Wilson, his cub reporter, in some disgust.

'So that's all you got out of the Mason business?' he asked shortly. 'I thought there would be more to his disappearance than that!'

Wilson shrugged. 'Don't blame me, boss, I did all I could. I tracked Mason from here to a dump called Craven Town, and after that to a shack — a filthy old hole. And did the place hum! There's a chemical dyeworks near there and the reek from that chimney of theirs is worse than glue. Smells like a grave or sump'n. It only stopped when the wind changed round.'

'Never mind that,' the editor returned coldly. 'What's all this about a red stain? Did you find that devil Gorne?'

'Sure — in the gorge below, with the living lights knocked out of him. There were two corpses buried near his shack, but it seems that in one of the graves he had unknowingly punctured a dye-pipe leading to the works and the darned stuff leaked out and coloured the ground crimson. There was a party of dyeworks men there when I arrived. I got the story from them. That's all there is to it.'

Danvers shrugged. 'Okay, then, but I expected something more interesting. At least we have it fairly clear that Mason and his daughter were murdered by this old lunatic Gorne. We'll print it. Hey, copy boy!'

THE END

Books by John Russell Fearn
in the Linford Mystery Library:

CLIMATE INCORPORATED
THE FIVE MATCHBOXES
EXCEPT FOR ONE THING
BLACK MARIA, M.A.
ONE STEP TOO FAR
THE THIRTY-FIRST OF JUNE
THE FROZEN LIMIT
ONE REMAINED SEATED
THE MURDERED SCHOOLGIRL
SECRET OF THE RING
OTHER EYES WATCHING
I SPY . . .
FOOL'S PARADISE
DON'T TOUCH ME
THE FOURTH DOOR
THE SPIKED BOY
THE SLITHERERS
MAN OF TWO WORLDS
THE ATLANTIC TUNNEL
THE EMPTY COFFINS
LIQUID DEATH
PATTERN OF MURDER
NEBULA
THE LIE-DESTROYER
PRISONER OF TIME

MIRACLE MAN
THE MULTI-MAN
THE RED INSECTS
THE GOLD OF AKADA
RETURN TO AKADA
GLIMPSE
ENDLESS DAY
THE G BOMB
A THING OF THE PAST
THE BLACK TERROR
THE SILENT WORLD

We do hope that you have enjoyed reading this large print book.

Did you know that all of our titles are available for purchase?

We publish a wide range of high quality large print books including:
Romances, Mysteries, Classics
General Fiction
Non Fiction and Westerns

Special interest titles available in large print are:
The Little Oxford Dictionary
Music Book, Song Book
Hymn Book, Service Book

Also available from us courtesy of Oxford University Press:
Young Readers' Dictionary
(large print edition)
Young Readers' Thesaurus
(large print edition)

For further information or a free brochure, please contact us at:
Ulverscroft Large Print Books Ltd.,
The Green, Bradgate Road, Anstey,
Leicester, LE7 7FU, England.
Tel: (00 44) 0116 236 4325
Fax: (00 44) 0116 234 0205

S.T.A.R. FLIGHT

E. C. Tubb

The Kaltich invaders are cruelly prolonging their Earthmen serfs' lives and denying them the secret of instantaneous space travel, so desperately needed by a barbaric, overpopulated Earth. While the Kaltichs strip Earth of its riches, the Secret Terran Armed Resistance movement, STAR, opposes them — but it's only their agent, Martin Preston, who can possibly steal the aliens' secrets. If he fails, billions of people will starve — with no place to go to except to their graves.

THE SILENT WORLD

John Russell Fearn

Around the world there was total silence from Pole to Pole. Seas crashed noiselessly on rocky shores, hurricanes shrieked mutely across the China Sea. People shouted and were not heard; alarms and bells rang and yet were mute. The dead wall of silence was everywhere — the most strident sound was unable to break through it. Scientists were unprepared for The Silence. There was something amiss with the laws which governed sound — but that was only the beginning . . .

DOUBLE ILLUSION

Philip E. High

Earth — four hundred years from now — a rotten society in which mankind is doomed to die out — and one seemingly average man with incredible I.Q. potential . . . An ultra-intelligent computer is built and used to govern humanity — and all corruption in the world is eradicated. Mother Machine decides what's best for her human children — and it is done. But the all-powerful computer is turning mankind into zombies. The world's only hope lies in one outlawed, not-so-average man . . .

A WOMAN TO DIE FOR

Steve Hayes

When hard-nosed PI Mitch Holliday loses his licence, he helps his partner, Lionel Banks, to pick up a missing girl named Lila Hendricks. But everything goes wrong; Mitch is drawn into a world of money, murder and double-cross. Seduced by socialite Claire Dixon's wealth — murder is now the name of the game. The target is a wealthy businessman with few redeeming qualities. Would Mitch, tough and cynical as he is, kill for the promise of love and money?

MEET JIMMY STRANGE

Ernest Dudley

Jimmy Strange was a mysterious young man who'd turn up when he was least expected; wherever there was trouble, he'd appear from behind some dark corner. No one knew much about him, though he was always a gentleman. He was never short of money, but where it came from no one knew. He wasn't a crook — yet they did say he could break into a house with the best of them — but always in a good cause . . .

SIX STRANGE CASES

Rafe McGregor

Private investigator Titus Farrow is doomed by an encounter with the Chambers Scroll; Roderick Langham solves the mystery of the 'Demeter' from his armchair by the sea; a failed author goes in search of the barghest for inspiration; a missing person case turns even nastier than blackmail; Sweeney Todd meets his match . . . These stories make a gripping journey through 'The King in Yellow', 'Dracula', 'Sweeney Todd', and the noir fiction of the pulp era.